To dear Josi
with much love
from Carol.

Christmas 1985

D1326053

J. H. WARBURG
19 WHITELEY ROAD
LONDON SE19 1JU
ENGLAND
01-670-5010

THE AMADEUS QUARTET

THE AMADEUS
QUARTET
The Men and the Music

Daniel Snowman

 Robson Books

FIRST PUBLISHED IN GREAT BRITAIN IN 1981
BY ROBSON BOOKS LTD., 28 POLAND STREET,
LONDON W1V 3DB. COPYRIGHT © 1981 DANIEL
SNOWMAN.

British Library Cataloguing in Publication Data
Snowman, Daniel
  The Amadeus Quartet.
  1. Amadeus Quartet
  I. Title
  785'.06'2421   ML1131

  ISBN 0-86051-106-5

Printed in Hungary.

CONTENTS

FOREWORD

The two principal dangers in writing about artists currently before the public are of steering too close to either the Scylla of producing cloying and premature obsequies or the Charybdis of writing *Hamlet* without the aid of the prince. I will not pretend that it was easy trying to steer a course between these two menaces as I prepared this book about the Amadeus Quartet.

All four members of the Quartet gave me the most unstinting co-operation and, sometimes at great personal inconvenience, did all they could to enable me to investigate in detail every aspect of their separate and collective lives and careers. I met them separately and together, recorded countless hours of conversation with each of them, watched them rehearse and perform at home and abroad, met their wives and families, browsed unimpeded through photo albums and even diaries, and felt free to ask any of them anything.

But this exceptionally warm-hearted co-operation from the Quartet could by no means have been guaranteed from the outset and, indeed, reflected considerable courage on their part – after all, they did not have the reassurance of knowing me when the project was mooted. Nevertheless none of them showed the slightest inclination to impinge upon my editorial independence.

My hope is that the book in its final form is neither gratuitously critical of the Amadeus Quartet nor so blandly appreciative as to render them unrecognizable to those who know and love them as they really are.

In addition to Norbert, Sigi, Peter and Martin and members of their families, I would like to register my gratitude to the following for their

7

help and advice: John Amis; Beryl Ball; Alan Blyth; Margot Bor; Robert Cahn; Levon Chilingirian; Hugo Cole; Sir Clifford Curzon; Margaret and Christopher Driver; Brigitte (Loeser) Eisner; Carl F. Flesch; W. W. French; David Gerver; Sir William Glock; Inge Heichelheim; Imogen Holst; Emanuel Hurwitz; Lord James of Rusholme; Robin Johnson; Hans Keller; Robert Layton; Lorna Letcher; Adrian Levine; Lisa Maclay; Michael Macleod; Wilfrid Mellers; Steven Paul; Maurice and Hilde (Beal) Pearton; William Pleeth; Dolf Polak; Wilfred Ransom; Ferdinand Rauter; Samuel Rhodes; Max Rostal; Harold Shukman; Ronald Stent; Rosamund Strode; Emmie Tillett; David Waterman; John West-Taylor; and to Dannie Abse whose idea it first was.

January 1981   DS

INTRODUCTION

They march on to the platform in reverse order, Martin Lovett, the tallest man with the tallest instrument, down to the shortest with the shortest. They acknowledge the applause as though slightly surprised by it, and bow – not as an ensemble but each with his own rhythm. They sit down and tune their instruments. An expectant hush falls over the packed audience. Bows hover over strings. And then, with absolute unity of control and unanimity of purpose, they launch into their opening work. Four very different men who sink – or transcend or incorporate – their differences into the greater whole.

To the extreme left and right, two generous crowns of now greying hair; in between, two balding domes. First, Norbert Brainin, rotund, ungainly, his thick mop of hair and powerful, pugnacious chin almost obscuring between them his determined facial features – an effect redoubled when, in passionate passages, he lifts his violin neck and bow up to head level. Yet from this stocky figure there flows a steady stream of the most mellifluous sound – and a sense of leadership and authority that sets the tone for the whole ensemble. Next to him, hunched, scarcely moving his eyes or body, his fixed jaw the only visible sign of an iron constitution, sits Siegmund Nissel, an unassuming-looking man whose tranquil appearance belies an exceptionally powerful and articulate personality, a man of versatile aesthetic and intellectual tastes and accomplishments. It was Nissel who first hit upon the name 'Amadeus'. The instruments and their bearers get bigger. There is the sensitive Peter Schidlof, a tall, distinguished-looking man with a long face who appears to embody all that was finest in the élite world of the old Austro-Hungarian nobility, though off-stage he can giggle mercilessly at upper-class pretentiousness. Trained on the violin, Schidlof, with his incomparable Macdonald Strad, is one of the finest viola players in the world. 'If you gave him a cigar box,' says Nissel appreciatively, 'Peter would still be able to coax from it the unique sound for which he is so famous.' Finally, Lovett, the one English-born member of the group and still visibly the youngest, yet long since completely integrated into the ensemble both musically and personally. In the early years, Lovett taught himself German so as not to be left out of the gossip – a decision that has paid dividends as the Quartet now spends so much of its time playing, recording and teaching in Germany. Lovett's wife, the violinist Suzanne Rozsa, knew Brainin, Nissel and Schidlof early since she, like them, was a student of Max Rostal.

The Quartet reaches the end of the final movement of the final piece. The applause is generous and the four men return to the platform several times to acknowledge it. A crowd of admirers and friends, well-wishers and autograph-hunters congregate backstage to shake hands, to embrace, to congratulate, to see, to be seen. The members of the Quartet deal graciously with all this attention. They are tired, and tomorrow are on their way again – to another city, another hotel, another audience, and another programme.

In this particular season they will play over one hundred concerts and over sixty different works. They are at home with their families for perhaps a total of four months out of twelve. A crazy life? Yes. But one to which they and their families have long ago had to adjust. For this is the Amadeus Quartet, for over thirty years at the pinnacle of one of the world's most demanding professions.

FIDDLERS THREE

'In prison' is where they like to say they met – or, at least, where Schidlof met first Brainin then Nissel. All three had recently managed to escape from Hitler, teenage Jewish refugees who wanted nothing more than to be left alone to play the violin. But within a year and a half of their arrival on British soil, war broke out and the three boys, in common with thousands of other German and Austrian nationals resident in the United Kingdom, found themselves rounded up and interned as 'enemy aliens'.

Internment was a typically British display of well intentioned slap-dashery. The Government had to be satisfied that the refugee community it had accepted – some 70,000 Germans and Austrians at the outbreak of war – did not shelter agents of the Third Reich. The original intention was to intern all 'enemy aliens' on the Isle of Man and then, in due course, transport them to the Dominions in a steady flow. But the indiscriminate detention of thousands of people, most of whom had come to Britain to escape arbitrary internment rather than to seek it, began to prick the much-vaunted British sense of 'fair play' – particularly after one ship, the *Arandora Star*, carrying 1,500 internees to Canada, was torpedoed off the coast of Ireland. The deportation policy was relaxed, but it was a while before adequate procedures could be developed to grant official clearance to those internees – virtually all of them – who proved to have a clean bill of political health. And until such procedures were developed, Brainin, Schidlof and Nissel and all the rest were billeted in a variety of more or less civilized prisons – a tent city here, a group of commandeered hotels there, a converted mill in a third place.

Brainin's adaptation for two violins of the Mendelssohn Violin Concerto. Part of the first movement.

Norbert Brainin was the luckiest. He was sent to Prees Heath in Shropshire in August 1940 and was cleared and released within a couple of months – though not before meeting a young man then called Hans Schidlof. Brainin had taken his violin with him and remembers playing it wherever and whenever he could. One day, he was playing away by his tent (the Mozart A major Concerto, as he recalls) and, behind him, people crept up to listen. One of the most attentive of his fellow-prisoners was a tall, handsome young man with a long, aristocratic face and sensitive fingers. 'I, too, play the violin,' announced the stranger diffidently, when Brainin had finished. 'You do?' answered the exuberant Brainin, and immediately handed him his instrument. 'Here! Go on. Play!' Within no time, the two had become firm friends. Someone sent Schidlof a fiddle of his own a week or two later and from then on he and Brainin were inseparable.

They must have been a strange pair: short, chubby Brainin, with his will of steel, and tall, aesthetic Schidlof, sawing away at Brainin's two-violin adaptation of the Mendelssohn Violin Concerto (Schidlof playing the solo part and Brainin his single instrument reduction of the whole of Mendelssohn's orchestration) in that remote spot of England under the bleak conditions of wartime internment. Suspended in time, having just left behind everything they had grown up with and with no idea what the future would hold, each clung on to the one thing that he knew and loved: his music. The bond that was created in that unlikeliest of settings was to last a lifetime.

The official machine ground away clumsily and Schidlof's release did not come for many more months. At one stage he (like Brainin some time before) was removed briefly to Onchan in the Isle of Man where one of his fellow internees was Siegmund Nissel. Nissel's recollection of internment is fairly rosy – at one stage, in Douglas, Isle of Man, he was held in a hotel on the sea-front where his co-inmates included one of the great chefs of Europe, so that *cordon bleu* dinners were served nightly!

Throughout this difficult period, the main thing, for Nissel as for so many other talented Jewish youngsters from central Europe in these camps, was music. So many of the world's leading musicians – string-players in particular – come from a Jewish background – Heifetz, Huberman, Elman, Flesch, Oistrakh, Menuhin, Milstein, Zukerman, Perlman . . . the list is endless. Thus Brainin and Schidlof and Nissel (and many of their fellow internees in various parts of England) were following in a long and honourable tradition as they clung, through all the physical and emotional upheavals of the time, to their music-making.

Their backgrounds were similar but not identical. The Brainins were Viennese furriers who originated from a little Byelorussian village between Smolensk and Vitebsk. Brainin's father came to Vienna in about 1911, anxious to avoid the pogroms that were still rife, to escape military service for the Tsar, and to improve his prospects elsewhere. A few years later, when Austria and Russia found themselves on opposite sides in the Great War, he was temporarily interned as an enemy alien – a family tradition that his son Norbert was to uphold a generation later! There were no musicians in the family, nor any figures of particular cultural eminence, save perhaps Norbert's great-uncle Reuben, a distinguished early Zionist who had settled in Berlin later and was one of the founding fathers, albeit a controversial one, of modern Hebrew language and literature. Great-uncle Reuben visited Vienna from time to time and was held up to young Norbert as a figure to revere but, by and large, the Brainins of Vienna were content to go about their business in a quiet, efficient and honourable way and to avoid public attention or controversy.

In 1929, the thirteen-year-old Yehudi Menuhin made his Vienna début and the event created a sensation. Not only was Menuhin still so young but his sheer mastery was a tonic to all who heard him. The Brainins, although not especially musical, were caught up in the fever. They, too, had a talented young son (Norbert was six at the time) and he, too, seemed to show musical flair. He was a bright lad, could read and write at four, and could sing both the words and music of more or less anything that was sung to him. Perhaps he was destined for great things? On his seventh birthday, Norbert was given a quarter-sized violin and his cousin Max, ten years his senior, a clever boy who could turn his talents to Latin and mathematics as well as music, gave him his first lesson. For Norbert the violin was love at first sight. 'Most children grow up wanting to be engine drivers,' he says, wryly, 'and hardly any of them ever make it.' His eyes twinkle as he adds with characteristic assertiveness, 'But I grew up and became exactly what I said I would!'

A year later Norbert's father died and, for the whole of the rest of his childhood and adolescence, in Vienna and later in London, Norbert (as well as his younger brother and sister and their mother until her death in 1938) was supported by his uncles and the family fur business. The generosity of the Brainin uncles must have been put to the test from time to time as their determined nephew devoted every available minute of every day to his expensive obsession. By the time he was eleven he was already leader of his school orchestra and a pupil of Riccardo Odnoposoff, the talented young concertmaster of the Vienna Philharmonic who, at twenty, was in addition a professor at the Vienna Music Conservatorium. Another of Norbert's teachers in those early years was Salomon Auber, one of Vienna's most brilliant chamber musicians, a master pianist and cellist, a dab hand at both violin and viola, and an outstanding teacher. When Auber himself was unavailable he would sometimes place his young pupil in the care of his wife, Marie, a distinguished musician in her own right who had learned the piano from the legendary Théodor Leschetizky.

The teacher whom Norbert remembers from those days with the greatest affection, however, is Rosa Hochmann-Rosenfeld, whom he first knew as a client of his uncles' fur business. Rosa Hochmann (like Carl Flesch) had studied the violin with Jakob Grün, himself a former colleague of Joachim; her sentimental education was said to have included strictly private tuition from the teenage Artur Schnabel. Even then, in her late fifties, she was a powerful personality, and the twelve-year-old Norbert fell in love with her. Rosa was an excellent musician and taught Norbert two invaluable lessons. Firstly, she imbued him with the peculiarly 'Viennese' tradition of music-making which many consider to have become the hallmark of the Amadeus Quartet many years later. And, secondly, this perceptive lady was the first to introduce Norbert Brainin to string quartets. She would play the first violin, Norbert the second, Hugo Kauder, a fellow music teacher and composer, the viola, and someone else the cello, and this unlikely ensemble would work its way through some of the quartet repertoire. Norbert remembers coming face to face for the first time with the Mozart D minor Quartet (K 421) and not even being able to read it properly. But he thought he knew, in his mind's ear, how it ought to sound and even likes to say today that it was at that point, as he struggled against the odds to bring the Mozart D minor to life, that he first imagined the sort of sound the Amadeus Quartet was one day to make.

There was a third valuable service that Rosa Hochmann performed: she provided the bridge to the legendary Carl Flesch, by then living in London and reputedly the world's greatest violin teacher. In the spring of 1938, shortly after the death of Brainin's mother, Norbert was due to pack his fiddle and sail to England for lessons. Then Hitler decided to celebrate Norbert's fifteenth birthday (12 March 1938) by organizing the capitulation of Austria to the Third Reich and life for the young Brainin orphans, not to mention their uncles, suddenly became more precarious. Norbert couldn't simply leave for London now; there was no knowing if he'd ever be able to return. As it happened, one of his furrier uncles was in London at the time of the Anschluss, stayed, and a few months later, as a result of a contact with a friend of Lord Winterton, the whole family managed to get permission to emigrate to England. They landed, a forlorn little band with scarcely a word of English between them, on Christmas Eve, 1938. Norbert's arrival was not quite in the style he had expected a few months earlier. He was in England not as a student but as a refugee. Nevertheless, it was literally no more than a matter of days before he had contacted Flesch and in January 1939 lessons began.

Norbert had been placed in a boarding school in Leigh-on-Sea near Southend but had permission to ignore virtually all his ordinary school subjects (aided and abetted in this by the entire school staff) so that he could concentrate on his violin. Once a week, he would take the train to Fenchurch Street station and the underground to Finchley Road, whence he would walk to the home of the Master in Canfield Gardens and enter a different and rarefied world. There are many qualities that go to make a great teacher, and they are hard to define. Flesch had a lot to say about all the usual things such as fingering and bowing and so on, but so did every other violin teacher. Some of Flesch's students were in awe of him and this very veneration probably helped the more steely-nerved to play better. Brainin's memory (which is backed up by that of Carl Flesch Jr.) is that he simply placed himself with total commitment into Flesch's hands and that the teacher, accustomed to being treated with formal reverence verging on fear, found this directness and sincerity so refreshing that a special bond was created between them. 'I opened myself up to him like a grateful son,' Brainin recalls, 'relying on his goodwill – and he responded. The relationship was a bit like that of doctor and patient. Flesch would listen, diagnose whatever your problems were, and suggest a remedy which would have the merit of helping you to help yourself to improve.'

Flesch gave what almost amounted to master classes. That is, his pupils not only received individual tuition but could also attend, as observers and even occasional participants, the lessons of others. In this way, Norbert got to know fellow-students like Yfrah Neaman, Ida Haendel, and Suzanne Rozsa (irresistibly beautiful – and always accompanied by her mother). Rather than return to Leigh-on-Sea after his lesson, Norbert would always draw out his weekly visit to Canfield Gardens and absorb as much as he could from Flesch's sessions with other young violinists. Then, for the princely sum of one shilling and sixpence, he would treat himself to a three course meal at the Balsam Restaurant in Finchley Road (long since renamed the Dorice) and eventually, when all further delaying tactics had been exhausted, make for Fenchurch Street and Leigh-on-Sea.

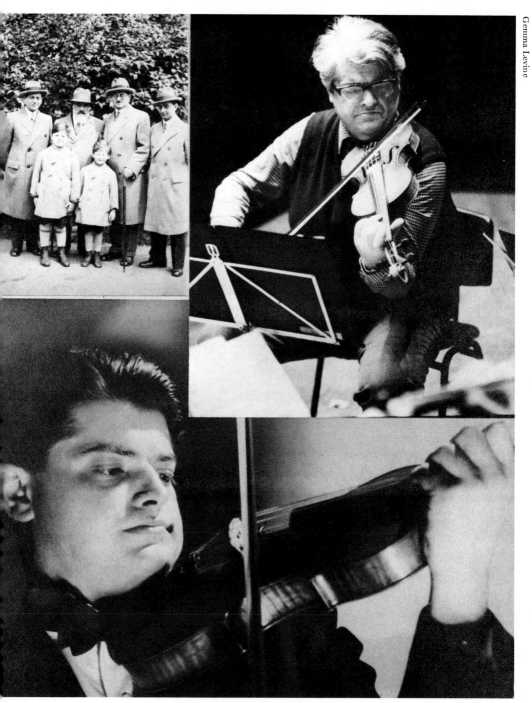

Norbert Brainin. Above left: *Norbert with his younger brother and great uncle Reuben (with beard).*

Gemma Levine

Siegmund Nissel.

In June 1939, Flesch went, as he generally did in the summer, to Knokke in Belgium. Many of his regular students, including Suzanne Rozsa, followed him there, but Norbert, only recently arrived in England and uncertain whether he'd ever be readmitted, did not dare run the risk. Master and pupil said goodbye and agreed to start lessons again in the autumn. But it was not to be. In late August, Flesch sent a postcard from Knokke saying that he would soon be leaving Belgium temporarily for what he considered the relatively safe haven of Rotterdam (where he only just survived one of the earliest major bombardments of the war). Flesch later made his way via his native Hungary across war-torn Europe to Switzerland, where he died in 1944 at the age of 71.

For Norbert Brainin, the onset of war brought in its train various benefits. For one thing, the farce of boarding school came to an end. No more caps and blazers and house ties, no more cricket and rugby. From now on, there was nothing to stop him from devoting himself entirely to music. Furthermore, the indefinite absence of Carl Flesch meant that Norbert came to be taught by his principal assistant, Max Rostal. Rostal was not only an outstanding violinist and a brilliant teacher in his own right, but was also destined to play an absolutely crucial role in the creation of the Amadeus Quartet. And a third by-product of the war was that, as things in Europe went from bad to worse to desperate, the *emigré* community in and around London developed an *esprit de corps* which rescued Norbert from what might otherwise have been a lonely life and enabled him to become a major star in a small but intensely responsive social and cultural firmament.

By the time he was interned in August 1940 and met Hans Schidlof, he had already established himself on the Hampstead-Highgate-Swiss Cottage circuit as a violinist to watch.

Schidlof was just a few months older than Brainin and although there were strong similarities in their background, the differences were at least as significant. Where Norbert was brought up in Vienna, Hans was from a small village of 200 houses in the wine country half way to the Czech border. Where Norbert attended a Zionist day school, Hans' parents sent him to a Roman Catholic boarding school. Where Norbert's first violin lesson was from a polymath cousin, Hans' was from the largely unlettered village blacksmith. Where Norbert knew from the age of seven that he wanted to be a musician, Hans' model was a cousin who had become a distinguished physical chemist. Where Norbert went on to study with the best music teachers in Vienna, Hans had to content himself with lessons from the school music teacher.

But the boys shared two things that would help to shape their common destiny: both were Jewish, and both played and loved music. For all Hans' apparent integration into the ambiance of his Catholic school (he was trotted out on occasion to perform before the Archbishop of Austria), the meaning of the Anschluss was as unmistakable for the Schidlof family as it was for the Brainins. Indeed Hans had always been uneasy at school and had felt himself called upon to excel just in order to keep at bay the anti-Jewish taunts of his fellows; so the arrival of a Nazi regime in Austria struck even more fear into his vulnerable heart than into that of Norbert, who was somewhat cosseted by his almost all-Jewish environment. Unlike Norbert, Hans was fortunate in having both his parents alive at the time of the Anschluss and they lost no time in arranging for Hans and his sister to leave Austria while the going was good. Like Norbert, Hans arrived in England in December 1938. Unlike Norbert, he had no connections there, so he and his sister were promptly dispatched to a school (St. Felix's in Southwold) for further processing.

Hans had never set foot outside Austria before, didn't know a word of English, and had temporarily lost touch with his parents. But he did carry a fiddle with him and very soon after he arrived he played a concert at his new, temporary school and was heard by Stephanie Hess, the sister of the music teacher at St. Felix's and herself an accomplished violinist. She managed to get the gifted youngster transferred on a special music scholarship to Blundell's School at Tiverton in Devon.

The long, slow, mid-winter train journey across England to Devon imprinted itself upon Hans' impressionable young mind. England looked interminable and dreary – but at least it seemed relatively safe from Hitler. This melancholy mood was modified a little by the kindness that Hans experienced from the people at Blundell's. Mr French, his generous-spirited housemaster, introduced him as gently as he knew how to the rigours and routines of public school life – early morning runs, stiff white collars, straw hats, games of rugger in which people seemed to be licensed to kick you in the stomach so long as they then said 'sorry' . . . 'I have seldom met a boy with a greater charm of manner,' wrote Mr French at the time, adding that Hans was 'extremely popular with the other boys on account of his obvious sincerity and admired for his talent in music which absorbs most of his thoughts.' Hans' principal preoccupation was fostered by Mr Hall, the classics master, who loved music and literature and did his best to lift the spirits of the bewildered newcomer. It was from Mr Hall's record collection that Hans first became acquainted with Elizabethan music and the wonders of Purcell. The headmaster, Mr Gorton (who later became Bishop of Coventry), encouraged Hans and even gave him permission to practise instead of attending all his classes. One master offered to put up Hans' parents on his farm if a way could be found to bring them over. Hans, for his part, treated everyone with the utmost respect and courtesy and all his school reports attest to his charm, talent and popularity. But he was an independent-minded boy, determined to go ahead with his music, and uneasy in his total reliance upon all these well-intentioned benefactors.

When war broke out in September 1939, Hans was suddenly an 'enemy alien'. He had to leave Blundell's; for a while, he boarded with Stephanie Hess, then he lived briefly in Kensington Gardens Square. Briefly, because the inevitable knock on the door followed in due course and he was taken off to Ladbroke Grove Police Station and thence ('Don't forget your tennis racket,' added a friendly policeman) to internment. It was at the police station that he first met the pianist Ferdinand Rauter who befriended him and was later instrumental in getting him released and introducing him to Max Rostal. At first, Hans (like Rauter) was sent to Prees Heath in Shropshire where he met Norbert Brainin; then he was billeted in a huge, dusty, rat-filled converted cotton mill near Bury, Lancashire. Finally he was transferred to various locations on the Isle of Man. In one of these, in Onchan, he met Siegmund Nissel, as well as many other musicians from central Europe. While 'in jail', Hans still received news from the outside world. He occasionally and irregularly heard from his parents (whose letters, greatly delayed, were re-routed through Switzerland). And he heard that his place in Kensington Gardens Square had been demolished in an early air raid. Above all, he heard on the camp radio the day-to-day news of the Battle of Britain and was able to follow the slow transformation of the situation in Britain's favour.

Hans was eventually released after a full year of internment, and only then with the active help of his former benefactress Stephanie Hess, as well as the newly-formed Musicians Refugees Committee, whose members included Ferdinand Rauter, Myra Hess, Ralph Vaughan Williams and Harriet Cohen. Why it took the British authorities a whole year to establish that this teenage Jewish musician did not constitute a security threat will never be known, but Schidlof finally got out of camp and shortly afterwards moved in with Hans and Kristin Berge, the former of whom he had met in camp, and with their mutual friend Siegmund Nissel.

19

One of Hans Schidlof's letters to his guardian, Stephanie Hess, written from Onchan internment camp and opened by the official censor before it ever reached her. It reads: I was very glad to have your letter from the 1st of January and I was very surprised about the telegram, which I received on Monday evening. Anyhow I do know now that my relations in America are still alive and I very much appreciate their willingness to help. I do not think the affidavit will be of very much use to me for it is not possible to get a shipping card. I got a letter today from Mr Ferdinand Rauter. He was interned and has been released, knows me very well. He is the accompanist of Engel Lund, a quite prominent musician. He writes I shall let him know all the particulars about my musical and school training. He believes he can do something for me. Sunday's concert was a success. Bach went very well. I am now going through the César Franck Sonata with Prof. Salomon. I am very well indeed and looking forward to meet you again. Please give my kind regards to your sisters. Yours sincerely, Hans.

Nissel had been born in Munich, but his parents were from Vienna and the traditions in which he had been raised were similar to those in the Brainin and Schidlof families. Like the other two, Sigi's violin-playing began early – at the age of six in his case. For three years he learned from various *ad hoc* teachers: his best friend's elder brother, a local nun, the leader of the Munich Radio Orchestra (who sapped Sigi's young ego by dozing as his pupil played). Sigi's parents encouraged him in his youthful interest. They were lower middle class Viennese Jews of Czech and Hungarian origins who had moved to Munich to try to improve their prospects, energetic and resourceful people who recognized talent and determination when they met it. Nissel's father had trained as a silver-smith and became managing director of a cutlery firm while his wife built up a little tailoring business and, in Sigi's early years, employed a dozen or more girls to help her. These were the years of Germany's economic depression and Sigi still remembers the tension in the streets of Munich as the Nazi Party – whose headquarters were just around the corner from his parents' apartment – began to feed off the discontent and grow into a serious menace.

In 1931, when Sigi was nine, Frau Nissel died, and his father took him 'back' to Vienna. There his violin playing continued. One of Sigi's teachers was Professor Max Weissgärber who had his own string quartet and was a member of the Vienna Philharmonic Orchestra. But it was still all rather casual, Sigi not yet certain that he wanted to pursue music as a serious career and his father harbouring more conventional career aspirations for him.

As with Brainin and Schidlof, the arrival of the Nazis in Vienna in March 1938 threw everything in Sigi's life out of kilter. Its first effect was to persuade his father that since being a Jewish doctor or lawyer was out of the question under the Third Reich, fiddle playing might be worth pursuing as a professional career after all. But, as it rapidly became obvious that being a Jewish anything under the Third Reich was a dubious proposition, the Nissels realized that the only thing to do was to get out. In the winter of 1938–9, two children's transports sailed for Britain carrying refugee children from Hitler's Reich. The first was met by voluntary organizations which processed the arrivals and alotted them to various families, schools, locations. The second, which sailed in January 1939, contained only children with guarantors already in Britain. If Hans Schidlof had not been on the first ship he would never have been allowed to board the second. Nissel, however, was fortunate in that Fritz Fleischer, his best friend in Vienna, was already in England staying with the Klinkart family in Ham in Surrey – and Fritz persuaded the Klinkarts to act as guarantors for young Sigi. For a while, Sigi and Fritz lived with the Klinkarts and did domestic chores in return for their keep. But it was an unsatisfactory situation that could not last.

Sigi was desperate to get his father out of Vienna before it was too late. This was not easy. Despite the already massively documented brutalities of the Nazis against the Jews, the British and American and other supposedly liberal-minded governments, still reeling from economic depression, were loth to admit more than a tiny handful of refugees from Hitler. Children aroused special sympathy, but even they were admitted in strictly limited numbers. Any adult liable to be an economic burden on the state was most unlikely to get in – but there was some chance if you could show either that you had money or moneyed friends, or that your real intention was to move elsewhere as soon as possible. Now, it happened that in the mid-1930s one of Sigi's uncles had befriended a rich American on holiday and had later presumed upon this friendship to obtain an affidavit to go to the United States. Shortly afterwards, and before taking advantage of this kindness, the uncle had committed suicide. At this point, Sigi, a lad of 15, had written to the American, told him of his uncle's suicide, and begged for a similar affidavit to be issued in the name of his own father. A very long shot, but it worked. And it provided the basis on which Nissel's father was eventually able to apply for temporary entry into Britain – which he finally did, successfully, in the last days of August 1939. By the time his train steamed into Liverpool Street station, war was hours away.

Life had been extraordinarily depressing for Sigi during the months preceding war. Occasionally he had tried to lift his spirits by playing the fiddle but he was out of practice and, being also out of money, he had no teacher to help him back to the level of playing he had achieved in Vienna. Someone gave him an introduction to Carl Flesch but the meeting was inauspicious. Mrs Klinkart offered to drive him to his appointment with the great teacher but had an accident on the way so Sigi had to complete the journey by taxi, alone, terrified of arriving late. Flesch proved courteous but distant. Sigi played the Bach G minor Sonata and Flesch's first comment – doubtless intended as a form of encouragement though it did not sound like it – was 'Fine; now play me something really difficult.' Sigi didn't have much of a repertoire at the time but managed part of one of the Mozart concertos. 'You've got talent,' Flesch acknowledged loftily, 'but I'm about to go abroad and can't take you on myself. You can take lessons with my assistant, Max Rostal.' What sounded like a crumb (for the name meant nothing to Sigi at the time) later materialized as a banquet. But for the time being Sigi was totally demoralized. 'You can sit in on my class this afternoon if you like,' Flesch added as an afterthought, 'to get some idea of what you still have to learn.' In the class, a young girl gave a stunning account of the Chausson *Poème*; her name was Ida Haendel. The legendary Joseph Hassid, who was to die shortly afterwards while still in his twenties, was in that class too ('The greatest violin genius I've ever heard,' says Brainin) – and, possibly, though neither man is sure, Brainin himself. The musical treat was lost on Sigi who made his lonely way back to the Klinkarts. Shortly afterwards, Europe was at war and, with a sigh, Sigi locked up his musical aspirations in his violin case.

The world seemed to stand still that winter, 1939–40. There was war, and yet there wasn't. Perhaps things would be all right after all. Sigi did not have the will (or the money) to work seriously at his violin. But he did teach himself passable English and even took, and passed, his matriculation.

Then came Dunkirk and the fall of France. The Germans were poised over the Channel and the cry went up among the more nervous and inhospitable of British social and political circles, 'Intern the lot!' Britain's finest hour was Siegmund Nissel's darkest as he was taken off by the very authorities who had so recently granted him sanctuary and placed with other 'enemy aliens', most of them Jewish, in a detention camp. 'If the Nazis successfully invade England,' Nissel recalls thinking gloomily, 'we'll be handed to them on a plate.'

As Britain's fortunes turned, however, so, in time, did Sigi's. Like Schidlof, he remembers following the later stages of the Battle of Britain on the camp radio in the Isle of Man and keeping a scoreboard of gains and losses. Most important was his meeting with Hans Schidlof at Onchan, a special friendship that was to affect deeply the lives of each. But he also met many other cultured and talented people in camp – the composer Franz Reizenstein, the violinist Max Jekel, who gave him some lessons, and Hans and Kristin Berge. 'The brains of Europe were in those camps,' Sigi says today exuberantly; 'they were a real university!' Not quite, perhaps, but the roster of internees reads a little like a *dramatis personae* of Britain's post-war intellectual and cultural élite. It includes painters like Fred Uhlman and the Dadaist Kurt Schwitters; musicians like Hans Keller, Paul Hamburger, Hans Redlich, Peter Gellhorn and Peter Stadlen as well as Brainin, Nissel and Schidlof; and scientists and social scientists of the eminence of Hermann Bondi, Hans Eysenck, Max

Henry Fisher (later editor of the *Financial Times*) and Claus Moser – whose decision to become a statistician resulted from the experience of doing a census of fellow inmates at Huyton internment camp. For many, internment had all sorts of unexpected benefits, and for Siegmund Nissel, too, camp life had the effect of raising his wilting spirits and providing him with congenial and appreciative company.

Nothing so became Sigi's internment as the manner of his leaving it. A couple of people in the camp had contacts with Myra Hess and Max Rostal and wrote to them about him. There were forms to be completed and committees to convince. Eventually Sigi was released under the pompous category 'persons of eminent distinction who have made outstanding contributions to Art' – a category which, according to Ralph Vaughan Williams and the refugee committee on which he sat, accurately described the bewildered seventeen-year-old Nissel. Hans Schidlof soon followed, having pursued the same path, and shortly afterwards virtually everyone was released. Hans and Sigi were happy, free, and hoping against hope that the war would somehow soon be over and that their adopted country might finally accept them and become their home.

THE WOLF GANG

By 1942 Britain was no longer in imminent danger of invasion and had been joined in the war effort by Russia and then America. Despite various Allied reverses in the early part of the year, 1942 witnessed some of the most decisive turning points of the war: the Battles of Midway and Guadalcanal in which the Americans gave notice to the Japanese that

A page from Martin Cahn's guest book.

they could win the War in the Pacific, the second Battle of El Alamein which enabled the Allies to make massive landings in North Africa and thereafter to invade Italy, and the long German siege of Stalingrad which the Russians were eventually to repulse and thereby seize the initiative on the Eastern Front.

For German and Austrian Jewish refugees, wartime Britain in 1942 proved a better year than its predecessor. Siegmund Nissel immeasurably cheered by the encouragement and friendships he had experienced in camp, was now living near his friends Hans and Kristin Berge in North Wembley and, in time, Hans Schidlof moved there as well. All four went on to live in Streatham (and went, in time, to Upper Norwood where they all shared a flat and, later still, to Mill Hill). The close musical and personal ties that had developed in camp survived internment and all these changes of address. When Schidlof and Nissel went to live in south London they kept in close touch with their friend Norbert Brainin who was by then staying with relatives in Hampstead Garden Suburb. For one thing, they all found themselves involved in the same social and cultural network. People like Dr. Edward May, an enthusiastic amateur cellist who lived in Highgate, or Martin Cahn of St. John's Wood, would organize informal musical soirées to which talented members of the refugee community would be invited. It was probably at the homes of such people as May and Cahn and at music evenings arranged by the Freie Deutsche Kultur-bund, the Anglo-Austrian Music Society, and many similar *emigré* cultural groups, that the sense of common purpose that later flowered into the Amadeus Quartet first developed as Norbert, Hans, Sigi, Susi Rozsa and her friend Martin Lovett played together in various *ad hoc* permutations. Even more important, though, was the fact that Norbert, Hans and Sigi (as well as Susi a little later) were all students of Max Rostal.

The debt the three boys owed Rostal is inestimable. Without Rostal's generous help (he never took a penny from Nissel and Schidlof whom he knew to live off the most meagre resources), they simply would not have been equipped to launch themselves upon the distinguished joint career that was soon to follow. Rostal took the three of them right back to the fundamentals of string playing and gave them the most thorough ground-ing in their art that any of them had ever had or could ever have hoped to have. He still has vivid memories of that period. Norbert, Rostal recalls, was bubbling over with new ideas, experiments, questions, doubts, confusions even, not just about music but about everything in life that he touched. His basic musical gifts were obviously of the highest order, and the questioning, almost impulsive quality that Rostal sometimes detected

ANGLO-AUSTRIAN MUSIC SOCIETY

at Austria House, 28 Bryanston Square
W.1

on Sunday, 2nd April, 1944, at 4—5.30 p.m.

At Home

Host and Hostess:

Dr. HERMANN ULLRICH

Miss M. FFRANGCON-DAVIES

————

PETER GELLHORN   -   *Piano*

SIEGMUND NISSEL   -   *Violin*

PAMELA HIND   -   -   *'Cello*

WILL PLAY TRIOS BY

BEETHOVEN AND MOZART

————

Viennese Coffee will be on sale
after the Concert.

— — —

Tickets: 2/6 (2/- if purchased 7 days in advance)
Members or their guests only.

in the relatively immature approach of those days was gradually applied, under careful tutelage, to excellent account. Without something of that same constant search for alternative ways of doing things so evident in Norbert Brainin's musicianship, the Amadeus Quartet would never have been able to grow and develop as it was to do over the decades ahead.

Sigi by contrast was always a far more accommodating pupil, according to Rostal's recollection. Less inclined than Norbert to ask awkward questions, he digested what he was told, worked hard and conscientiously, and made enormous strides. Hans was in those days the most exuberant player of the three, wild even. 'He played everything with fantastic temperament,' Rostal remembers. 'He nearly cut the violin in half, over-pressed madly, and played with tremendous intensity.' He was the most difficult of the three for Rostal to 'tame' – quite a contrast to the beautifully controlled, almost restrained viola player the world came to know. All three players obviously were tremendously gifted musicians, and Rostal was proud of the progress they made.

At that time Rostal also ran a chamber ensemble and he used this to extend the experience of his more promising pupils. The set-up varied from one concert to the next. Sometimes Norbert or Hans would be asked to play the viola part. Peter recalls the first time he ever played the viola; it was in a Rostal Chamber Orchestra performance of the Bach Brandenburg Concerto No. 3, and he could not even read the viola clef when they first rehearsed the piece.

RECITAL 10

IN AID OF MRS. CHURCHILL'S FUND FOR RUSSIA·

by

FANNY WATERMAN   RENE SELIG
(Two Pianofortes)

NORBERT BRAININ
(Violin)

CITY MUSEUM, PARK ROW, LEEDS, I

SATURDAY, JANUARY 2nd, 1943.

Doors Open 6 p.m.   **1/6**   Commence 6-30 p.m.

There was a war on and everyone was expected to pull his weight, even budding musicians. To Brainin, Nissel and Schidlof, the essential thing was to stay close to Rostal. That meant finding war work in London which they could complete in the early afternoon in time to go on to their lesson. Norbert, although worried that he might do his hands some injury, took a job as an unskilled machine tool fitter ('So unskilled,' he says now, 'that it's a wonder we didn't lose the war!'). Sigi worked in a metal factory in the East End making brass and gun metal out of scrap. Hans trained as a dental mechanic. It was a difficult and tiring time. The three boys were each working for eight hours a day and then going on to do four more of music. Physical and mental candles were being burned at both ends, and, for all Rostal's generous tutelage, there must have been times when each of the boys wondered whether it was all worth while.

Norbert had the toughest time. He found himself in bad odour with the Home Office over the fact that he had received unauthorized payment (an occasional paltry guinea or two) for some of his refugee soirée appearances. Indeed, he was even reprimanded for giving those informal concerts in the first place, especially any that took him away from his 'essential' war work as an unskilled machine tool fitter. Nearly dismissed from his job Norbert became demoralized, the more so when he found that as a result of his job his forearm and shoulder muscles were tightening to the point that agile violin fingering became increasingly difficult. From about mid-1943, in fact, until the end of the war two years later, he played his violin less and less, preferring to mark time until something like normality should return.

Normality – or peace at any rate – returned in the summer of 1945 and Norbert, Sigi and Hans, in common with millions around the world, tried to pick up the pieces of their disrupted lives. Norbert also tried to pick up the violin again, found he was too stiff to hold a bow and, too embarrassed to go back to Rostal, simply applied himself with iron self-discipline to the task of working himself back into form. By 1946 he was appearing all over the place – a sonata concert here, an *ad hoc* chamber group there, and the occasional informal concerto appearance. Imogen Holst invited him to Dartington Hall, where she was music director, for a few weeks in the summer. One of the music staff at Dartington at the time noted in her diary that 'Norbert is dynamite – electrified everyone, including audience ... Does everything with whole of himself – eating, playing and laughing ... Everything he does, and is, is Gargantuan. Quartets for two hours and then reduced us to jellies of laughter with his "funny anecdots" ... Extraordinary playing – intense, burning but very controlled ... In that hall, with a few listeners, it was one of those occasions that sear into one's system.'

As a goal to help keep himself going, and as a sort of private homage to his great teacher who had died in 1944, Brainin decided to enter the second year of the Carl Flesch Gold Medal Award, in October 1946. After a year of agonizing hard work, the great day arrived. As it happened, he played the very piece – the Bach G minor Sonata – that Nissel had played to the Master himself seven years earlier, plus the Brahms Concerto. Norbert won first prize, and was overcome; his victory, as only he really knew, represented an extraordinary feat of mind over body. But the strain of competitive music-making had depressed him and he vowed never again to subject himself to that sort of pressure. His greatest fulfilment came from chamber work and for a while he played trios with Edmund Rubbra on the piano and the cellist William Pleeth. He also drifted back happily into the musical company that he had found so welcoming in the years just after his internment. He took up again with the Rostal Chamber Orchestra and tried his hand at the viola from time to time – sharing this double act with Schidlof (who was now more commonly called Peter). Sigi Nissel would often play with them too, and the music-making was always congenial. One day, Peter had a call from fellow Rostal student Suzanne Rozsa. She had to withdraw from a Wigmore Hall concert at which she and her young cellist friend Martin Lovett were due to play the first performance in England of the violin and cello duo by Honnegger. Could Peter stand in for her and do the violin part? He could. And so the two boys, who were destined to share so much of their lives, gave their first joint chamber concert.

Martin Lovett was still a teenager while the others were 22 or 23, but he had been a musician for almost as long as they had. His father, Sam Lovett, was a cellist; *his* father had been a violinist before going into business as an insurance broker and had bought his little grandson Martin a fiddle and shown him how to hold it. ('Does it hurt?' he'd ask. 'Yes? Good.') Sam Lovett's cello teachers had included William White-house, himself a pupil of the great virtuoso Piatti, and Herbert Walenn, the founder and principal of the London Violoncello School and the doyen of British cello teachers. One of his fellow students under Walenn was John Barbirolli. Times were hard in the Twenties and Thirties and Sam Lovett, like many another serious musician, found himself having to play in cinema and hotel orchestras and with popular bands like Geraldo and

Mantovani. The Lovetts moved around a lot: from Stoke Newington (where Martin was born in 1927) to Hendon for a few years; then out of London to Liverpool; back to London again; then off North once more, this time to Leeds. Most of the moves were connected with Sam Lovett's work and, although he loved music and the cello, he and his wife did not encourage their son to pursue a musical career. However, it became quite clear that Martin had an excellent ear and considerable talent so that when he announced at the age of eleven that he, too, intended to become a cellist, nobody demurred. Indeed, such were the boy's enthusiasm and ability that his father's initial scepticism soon turned to helpful encouragement. Martin remembers with great affection the way his father gradually introduced him to chamber literature and took him through some of the great quartets by means of *ad hoc* do-it-yourself cello duets.

In 1942, at the tender age of fifteen, Martin won a scholarship to the Royal College of Music in London where he shared with Alan Loveday and Hugh Bean the double distinction of being one of the youngest and also one of the most outstanding students of the time. At the college, where he first met Suzanne Rozsa, a fellow student, Martin received formal training in every aspect of music and musicianship (the only member of the Amadeus Quartet to have been so privileged). His cello studies were directed by Ivor James, the cellist in the Menges Quartet, and, still in his mid-teens and supposedly a full-time student, Martin was soon in demand as a semi-professional player by all sorts of small chamber groups. He played in occasional CEMA concerts for troops and factory workers, and still recalls trying his hand at quartets with various formidable German refugees 'who spouted Goethe at me!' War-time London provided a tough school for a youngster from the provinces, but Martin's energy and talent ensured that he would gain from the experience.

On completing his work at the Royal College in 1945, Martin simply switched gears and built up the freelance cello work that had already begun to flow his way. He stayed in London and did film and recording sessions, worked with various opera and symphony orchestras – and, whenever possible, played chamber music, appearing with the Rostal Chamber Orchestra which included all or some of his future Amadeus colleagues. Sam Lovett, meanwhile, had joined John Barbirolli's reconstituted Hallé Orchestra (and, later, the London Philharmonic of which he was to become sub-principal cellist, and Vice Chairman of the Board of Directors). Martin still recalls with special pleasure joining the Hallé on occasion and playing alongside his father.

Life for a talented young musician was full of exciting opportunities.

Martin went to hear all the major musicians of the time and remembers being particularly moved by the genius of Casals, whom he has always considered the greatest of all cellists – an impression that was to be reinforced years later when he came to know Casals and to play with and for him at Prades and Zermatt. In 1946 came a sudden call from Ernest Ansermet who was at Glyndebourne to conduct Britten's new *The Rape of Lucretia* and who needed a last-minute cello substitute. Martin Lovett went straight into the pit and sight read Britten's tricky score, much to the delight and surprise of the other members of the orchestra (including the violinists Emanuel Hurwitz and Peter Schidlof) and, above all, of Ansermet. Later in the year came the Honegger duo with Schidlof at the Wigmore Hall. And Martin was still in his teens when he became principal cellist in the Sadler's Wells Orchestra with whom he performed all the standard ballet and opera scores.

Norbert, Sigi, Peter and Martin all knew and appreciated each other's playing. Equally important, they were each coming to realize that what they did best and liked most was chamber music. It is unclear whose idea it was that they should get together as a quartet, though once they did there was total dedication from all four, a powerful communal impulse that led them to rehearse together six hours a day for the better part of a year. Norbert and Peter both played the viola as well as the violin and at first there was some talk of the two of them sharing violin and viola duties in piano and flute quartets and the like. But as the foursome got down to serious rehearsals together in early 1947, it soon became clear that, if they were to achieve a high standard of musicianship, this sort of chopping and changing was not possible, and Peter agreed to subordinate his principal instrument to the less familiar one.

Nobody knew what direction the new working partnership would take. They didn't even have a name. When Imogen Holst invited them down to give a concert in the Banqueting Hall at Dartington in the summer of 1947, they performed as the 'Brainin String Quartet'. And what a concert they gave! It consisted of three of the most demanding works in the quartet repertoire: Mozart's D major, K 499, Schubert's *Death and the Maiden* and Beethoven's Razumovsky No. 3. The Dartington appearance was a great success. 'Really exciting,' wrote one listener at the time. 'Still rough and unpolished, but dynamic.' Imogen Holst was deeply moved. Brainin, in particular, she felt, was one of the people to give her the most profound musical insight since her father, Gustav Holst, had died

Peter Schidlof. Below: *Peter as a schoolboy at Blundell's.*

Martin Lovett.

Above left: *A Bryanston cabaret with Schidlof playing Brainin's violin and Lovett on the piano.* Above right: *The Quartet with Cecil Aronowitz, Scheveningen, early 1950s.* Below: *Early days together at Bryanston.*

George Enesco with (above) *the Quartet and* (below) *Suzanne Rozsa.*

Great Hall - Dartington Hall

13th JULY, 1947

BRAININ STRING QUARTET

Norbert Brainin (Violin)   Peter Schidlof (Viola)
Siegmund Nissel (Violin)   Martin Lovett (Violoncello)

PROGRAMME.

Quartet in D major, K.499   Mozart
    Allegretto
    Menuetto - Allegretto
    Adagio
    Allegro

Quartet in D minor, Op. Post.   Schubert
    Allegro
    Andante con moto
    Scherzo - Allegretto molto
    Presto

Quartet in C major, Op. 59, No. 3   Beethoven
    Introduzione - Andante con moto
              Allegro vivace
    Andante con moto quasi allegretto
    Menuetto - Grazioso
    Allegro molto

PRIZE MEDAL 1862.

SOLE GOLD MEDAL
SOCIETY OF ARTS 1885.

GOLD MEDAL
INVENTIONS EXHIBITION 1885.

GOLD MEDAL
PARIS UNIVERSAL
EXHIBITION 1889.

DIPLOME D'HONNEUR
BRUSSELS INTERNATIONAL
EXHIBITION 1897.

WEMBLEY 1924.

ALBERT PHILLIPS HILL.
PAUL EBSWORTH HILL.
DESMOND D'ARTREY HILL.

17th Feby 1660 *"In ye morning came Mr. Hill ye Instrument Maker, and I consulted with him about ye altering my lute and my viall."*
Pepys Diary.

23rd May 1789 *My Amati wanted glueing so took it to Hill's for necessary repairs.*
From a Diary by Thomas Lewin.

William E. Hill & Sons,

140, New Bond Street,

LONDON. W.1.

23rd July, 1947.

Mrs. Leonard Elmhirst,
Dartington Hall,
Totnes,
Devon.

Dear Mrs. Elmhirst,

I thank you for your letter of the 21st and appreciate your desire to purchase a good violin for Mr. Brainin.

I most certainly agree with you that he is a violinist of outstanding ability and he strikes me as having quite exceptional musical interpretation which is so lacking in many players who are in other respects good violinists.

The violin which he liked most is one made by Pietro Guarnerius of Venice. The lowest figure that we could accept for this would be £1250 (one thousand two hundred and fifty pounds) and in view of your letter we should be pleased to let Mr. Brainin take it away to give it a thorough trial and will communicate with him to this effect.

Yours truly,

A. Phillips Hill

thirteen years earlier. When Leonard and Dorothy Elmhirst, the wealthy and idealistic founders of the Dartington community, school and cultural centre, heard from Imogen Holst that Brainin's small Amati violin was borrowed for the occasion, they sent him off to W. E. Hill's, the violin dealers, where he chose a Pietro Guarneri of Venice for which they paid (a bill of £1,250). As for Imogen Holst, herself a person of great generosity though without the financial resources of the Elmhirsts, she was so impressed by the foursome that she offered, out of her own pocket, to underwrite their professional début. The Quartet was to book the Wigmore Hall the following January and launch itself with all due pomp and circumstance in London. And she would put down what was then the not inconsiderable sum of £100 to cover the basic expenses.

Throughout that autumn, the foursome rehearsed continuously, and tried out their fast developing skills as an ensemble before their friends. A fortnight before the posters and leaflets were due to be prepared for the Wigmore début the Quartet had still not decided upon its permanent name. The 'Brainin Quartet' did not sound quite right. Norbert Brainin was not at that time a well known figure in the musical world comparable to Adolf Busch or Sidney Griller with their eponymous quartets, and in any case the habit of adopting a non-personal name – the Aeolian and Pro Arte were good examples – seemed more in tune with the times. Furthermore, the Quartet had only come into being because Peter had sacrificed his own aspirations to a career as a violin soloist – and even perhaps a quartet leader – to the greater interests of the foursome as a whole; it might have been insensitive to have endowed the group permanently with the name of the man for whom he felt he had made that sacrifice. Geographical names were 'in' (though these could be misleading – all four members of the Budapest Quartet were Russian!), and for a while they thought of themselves as the 'London-Vienna Quartet'. But that did not last long. 'Sounds too much like a railway timetable,' snorted one, and the rest agreed. Nissel proposed 'Amadeus'. It sounded nice, embraced the ideas of love and God, and was Mozart's middle name. 'Ridiculous,' came the inevitable first reactions. 'They'll think that all we can play is Mozart!' – a problem that was later to dog quartets like the Borodin, Smetana, Berg and Bartok. The debate went back and forth. Other names were suggested and dropped. But 'Amadeus' kept resurfacing, like an insistent rondo theme. 'OK,' they agreed, a day or two before the posters had to be printed, 'let's be the Amadeus String Quartet and the hell with it!'

The result of Imogen Holst's generous gesture of faith has become

WIGMORE HALL

WIGMORE STREET, W.I

THE

AMADEUS
STRING QUARTET

NORBERT BRAININ *(Violin)*   **PETER SCHIDLOF** *(Viola)*

SIEGMUND NISSEL *(Violin)*   **MARTIN LOVETT** *('Cello)*

SATURDAY AFTERNOON
JANUARY 10th, 1948
at 3 p.m.

TICKETS (including Tax):   Reserved 9/- and 6/- ;   Unreserved 3/-

(All bookable in advance)

May be obtained from BOX OFFICE, WIGMORE HALL (WEL. 2141), usual Ticket Offices and

IBBS & TILLETT LTD., 124, Wigmore Street, W.I

Telephone: Welbeck 2325 (3 lines)

Telegrams: "Organol, Wesdo, London."

Hours : 10—5. Saturdays, 10—12

Ticket Office : Welbeck 8418

Vail & Co., Ltd., E.C. (1947)

For Programme P.T.O.

musical legend. On the afternoon of 10 January 1948, the queue outside the Wigmore Hall for the ensemble's début stretched down the street and around the block. For those lucky enough to gain admission the concert was a feast of great music magnificently played. The Quartet started, appropriately, with one of the most powerful chamber works of Mozart: the D minor, K 421; they followed this with the Verdi (the performance of which difficult work 'placed this quartet right at the top of the tree technically, intellectually and musically,' said the London music critic of *The Scotsman*); and they brought the proceedings to a triumphant close with Beethoven's Razumovsky No. 3, which even the sober *Times* had to acknowledge was played 'robustly [but] without roughness or neglect of minutiae'. In addition to all the usual critics, the BBC were there, talent scouts for the brand new Third Programme, and they immediately approached the Quartet with broadcasting offers.

A full programme, a packed house, and favourable reviews in all the right places – no young group could have hoped for a more successful début. Why, in addition to the basic fact that they obviously played well, did things go quite so unerringly their way? Why, indeed, were so many people in the first place fighting to hear a group with virtually no record of public achievement behind it? Part of the answer is suggested by the comment, in one review, that 'we must welcome their appearance warmly for the shortage of good quartets is acute'. The war had caused a serious hiatus in the musical life of London and by early 1948 the old threads were only just beginning to be drawn together again. Many of the great musicians of the 1930s were either dead or else no longer available for (or perhaps capable of) performances of pre-war standards. Most younger musicians of promise had just spent six years in uniform in conditions not exactly conducive to the highest standards of artistic excellence. If the Amadeus had been able to time their emergence on the scene they could not have chosen a better moment.

It is easy to forget, after the two or three decades in which London has been something like the musical capital of the world, how limited its musical life was by today's standards back in the 1930s and how severely the onset of war affected the quality (if not the quantity) of London's musical offerings still further. International opera in the Thirties was normally represented by a two-month season of Italian and German opera at Covent Garden each spring plus the occasional visiting company from abroad. This operatic fare was kept going largely as a result of the genius and generosity of one man, Sir Thomas Beecham. Of today's major London orchestras, the BBC Symphony and the London Philharmonic (also a child of Beecham's artistic and financial generosity) were both less than ten years old when the war broke out, while the Philharmonia was still a thing of the future. The war itself threatened to reduce music-making to a shadow of its former self. A number of dedicated musicians – mostly those who were the wrong age or sex or nationality to fight – did sterling work in keeping an active musical life going in the capital and

NATIONAL GALLERY CONCERTS

FERDINAND RAUTER (*Pianoforte*)

PETER SHIDLOF (*Violin*)

Programme

I

Sonata in B flat, K. 454   *Mozart*

          Largo—Allegro
          Andante
          Allegretto

II

Sonata in D minor, Op. 108   *Brahms*

          Allegro
          Adagio
          Un poco presto e con sentimento
          Presto agitato

STEINWAY PIANOFORTE

Tuesday, August 7th, 1945   Price One Penny

elsewhere, while many of those in uniform, assisted by the Council for the Encouragement of Music and the Arts (CEMA), helped to keep up their own spirits and those of their comrades by performing to factory workers and to troops. The famous National Gallery concerts organized by Dame Myra Hess performed to something approaching a million people during and just after the war (and included among the distinguished roster of performers all four members of the future Amadeus Quartet).

These wartime musical activities played an important part in helping to build up audiences around the country and in bringing serious music to listeners who had never experienced it before. One violinist had an unexpectedly large audience at a military base – only to discover that the soldiers had misheard the name of the main attraction and had expected to hear, not the Franck Sonata, but Frank Sinatra. One may hope that they, like hundreds of thousands of other sceptical listeners attending their first concert of serious music in those years, stayed, and enjoyed. But for all the converts made to the cause by CEMA, for all the popularization of the classics that took place during the war, the musical scene was still bleak. There was, in sum, a lot of music about; but standards, whether of composing, programming, or performing, were inevitably very patchy and for those with cultivated tastes the picture was frankly appalling. The destruction of the Queen's Hall by a bomb on the night of Saturday 10 May 1941 was a symbolic as well as a literal loss; music-making in London would never, they said at the time, be the same again.

Enormous efforts were made after the war to capitalize on the new audiences that had been wooed by CEMA artists in the National Gallery and all over the country and to introduce them to the highest standards of pre-war music-making. Artists like Josef Szigeti, Yehudi Menuhin, Artur Schnabel and Elisabeth Schumann came to London for the first time in years (and often performed in either the Wigmore Hall which was too small or the Royal Albert Hall which was too large); Covent Garden was converted back into an opera house again having been a dance hall during the war, while at Sadler's Wells they staged the première of one of the indubitable operatic masterpieces of modern times, *Peter Grimes*, by the young English composer Benjamin Britten; in 1946 the Arts Council of Great Britain was established to take up where CEMA had left off and to use public funds to encourage the arts, while wise men at the BBC set up a new radio network entirely devoted to cultural matters – and, in particular, to music. It was a time of promise rather than fulfilment, of anticipation among the young and some nostalgia among those who were a little older. Nobody foresaw the tremendous leap into musical prominence that London would take over the next ten or twenty years and it was still a matter of self-congratulation if a young British musician – a Kathleen Ferrier, say, or a Dennis Brain – was seen to reach the highest international standards. But it could be done, and the very excitement that greeted home-grown achievement of this kind was testimony to the inadequate offerings with which wartime England had of necessity to content itself.

The chamber music world was a particularly untended wilderness. There were plenty of good instrumentalists around and, since chamber music was cheap and therefore attractive to promote, many of the best players had been heard in London and the provinces during and just after the war. But the bad mingled with the good and often drove it out, halls were often half filled, acoustically poor and draughty, and the highest standards of professional ensemble playing were hard to find. The Busch Quartet's days were drawing to a close and its appearances in Britain rare. The Grillers were about to move to the United States thus denying London one of the best of its home-grown ensembles. There was a thirst for good chamber music, but a paucity of groups really capable of providing it. Thus, when word spread around musical London that a new quartet was forming, there was already an eager audience for the Amadeus to tap.

There was an additional reason why this particular ensemble was capable of attracting a sell-out audience at its début. While the Amadeus Quartet was not yet known as such, each of its members had by now accrued a considerable following. Ever since the musical soirées of the war years, all four members had been well known in musical circles. And the wartime *esprit de corps* of the refugee community was still strong so that there was almost a parental pride among many who saw the names of their young friends on the posters that sprouted in and around London at the end of 1947. 'Do you remember those talented boys whom we heard playing at Eddie May's and Martin Cahn's and at Anglo-Austrian musical evenings?' people said. 'Well, they've formed themselves into a professional quartet. We really ought to go and help launch them.'

Launched they well and truly were, and the voyage has been at full speed almost continuously since. Within the first year the Quartet was already appearing throughout Britain. Like all talented beginners who happen to be in the right place at the right time, they also had their fair share of good luck. In March 1948 they eagerly took over when the Hungarian String

Quartet cancelled an engagement in Bradford; later in the year, in Birmingham, they stood in when Poulenc and Bernac had to cancel a concert owing to the indisposition of the latter (and then had the temerity to play not only Mozart and Verdi but also a quartet by the virtually unknown Priaulx Rainier); when the Busch Quartet had to bow out of an engagement sponsored by the wealthy Cornwall-based Thai patron of the arts, Prince Chula Chakrabongse, it was the Amadeus who took over. They toured South Wales; they appeared at William Glock's first summer school at Bryanston (where Imogen Holst recalls rehearsing them in unfamiliar Purcell) and later performed the Mozart piano quartets with Glock (Schidlof playing violin and Brainin viola); and – a sure way of learning the quartet repertoire – they were constantly in demand for broadcasts (all live) and always invited to play a new programme.

The overwhelming and immediate success of the new group put to rest any question of how full time it was likely to be. All four knew that they would be foolish to let any other forms of musical activity stand in its way. There were teething difficulties, of course, but most things fell into place fairly painlessly. The musical division of labour was finally settled as Schidlof, no doubt encouraged by many reviews that singled out his viola playing for especial praise, eventually placed his fiddle firmly back in its case without too many regrets.

By the beginning of 1950, two years into its professional career, the Amadeus Quartet had established itself as one of the major ensembles of its kind. Friends affectionately nicknamed them the 'Wolf Gang', though a few critics (or typographers) who kept to 'Amadeus' were not yet universally familiar with their individual names; a Mr Norbert Braidin made an occasional appearance with them, not to mention a Mr Peter Semidlof, while the French press persisted in calling the cellist 'Martin Lowett'. Audiences were occasionally a little sparse in those early days, especially if the Quartet included a work by a contemporary composer or visited some relatively out-of-the-way spot. But the second anniversary of their professional début found the group off to Scotland for a busy tour, itself something of a warm-up for their first trip abroad, to Spain in March. Then, in June, a further foreign tour, this time to a country that had already played a pivotal role in the lives of three of them but was also destined, with supreme irony, to become almost a second home to the Quartet – Germany. Great new horizons were opening up for the Amadeus, and beyond them new worlds beckoned.

Despite its early successes, life for the Amadeus Quartet in the 1950s was not one of unalloyed luxury. At concerts, the players could enjoy the comfortable illusion that they had the world at their feet. But that world was a small and select one. Outside the somewhat *recherché* confines of the chamber circuit, the Amadeus Quartet had to face all life's knocks without a benign employer or a pension or promotion prospects to cushion them. In the early days, they were lucky if they each got ten pounds a concert and even in the United States their fees were not high considering that the expenses involved in an extensive four-man tour could eat up two-thirds of their gross income. The time was still far in the future when an El Al steward would eagerly ask for their autographs and then discuss interpretations and even fingering with them, or when Ansett Airlines of Australia would feature Martin Lovett and his cello in their publicity magazine. Back in the early 1950s the foursome counted themselves privileged to obtain the strictly professional rewards that they did and learned to accept with resignation that the wider world would often assume that the Amadeus Quartet was some sort of jazz group. In an American hotel bar they idly passed the time with a man identifying himself as a fellow musician. 'Can you cats play?' he asked innocently.

By the time the Amadeus Quartet achieved its tenth birthday it had reached a point of fame and fortune that led it to embark upon an extended world tour. From a trans-continental trip across America they went on to Hawaii, thence to Japan, Hong Kong, New Zealand, Australia and South Africa, arriving home eight months, 40,000 miles and 145 concerts later. Everywhere they went they received ecstatic notices. The Japanese, in particular, were stunned by the brilliance of the Amadeus who, along with the imminent advent of the jet plane and modern recording techniques, were to prove a major force in opening up Japanese interest in Western music. By the time the Quartet returned to England at the end of August 1958, they had become stars. The British press welcomed them back, several papers featuring Lovett's discovery in Boston of a button-sewing machine ('just the thing for the wifeless traveller'), while the London *Evening News* photographed Nissel's reunion with his wife Muriel and his first glimpse of their baby girl, Claire, born when he was 12,000 miles away in New Zealand.

The Amadeus never had to hunt for work. From the earliest years offers regularly poured in and life for the Quartet was – and has been ever since – an almost uninterrupted whirl of concerts, broadcasts, foreign tours, recording sessions, festival appearances, and various summer and winter schools.

Дорогой друг - Мартин!
Я очень горячо поздравляю
Тебя с превосходной
игрой сегодня. Я очень часто
играл этот Квинтет с
разными виолончелистами,
но сегодня мне было
играть приятнее чем всегда.
Я весьма давно Тебя не слышал
(после Токио) и считаю что
Ты теперь играешь много
много лучше чем раньше.
Много думал о Твоём
прежнем нездоровье и
сегодня окончательно
убедился что болезнь
к Тебе больше не вернётся.
Я еще раз Тебя благодарю

з- удовольствие которое
Ты мне сегодня доставил
Буду счастлив еще
много, много, много
раз играть с Тобой
это Великое произведение
Всегда Твой
Слава

1964.
Алдебург
21/VI

A letter from Rostropovich to Martin Lovett written after the concert reads: Martin, my dear friend, I should like to give my warmest congratulations on your magnificent playing today. I have often played this quintet with different cellists, but it was a greater pleasure today than ever before. It is a long time since I heard you (in Tokyo) and consider that you are now playing very much better than before ... Thank you once more for the pleasure you gave me today. I shall be very happy to play this great work with you many, many times. Always your Slava. Rostropovich.

There have been highlights, of course. Their regular attendance at the Dartington summer school was one such. The members of the Quartet have always had an especially soft spot for Dartington and are at their most exuberant and relaxed whenever they visit the superb old estate near Totnes where they met with so much kindness and encouragement at the outset of their collective career. In a letter to Leonard Elmhirst in 1953, Imogen Holst wrote: 'I like to think of the Standard Books of Musical History of the year 2053 mentioning Dartington and the Amadeus in the same sort of way that our present day histories mention Esterhazy and Haydn.'

By that time, Imogen Holst had moved to Aldeburgh to assist Benjamin Britten and Peter Pears in the planning of their annual festival there, and Aldeburgh, like Dartington, took on a special place in the affections of the Quartet. They played at the Festival almost every year in the Fifties and Sixties, performed the Mozart piano quartets in 1956 with Britten playing an old fortepiano, and gave the Schubert C major Quintet in 1964 with Rostropovich playing the second cello part.

On 7 June 1969, they inaugurated that year's Festival with what proved to be the last concert in the Maltings before the building burned down. Four years later they returned to the rebuilt Maltings for the Mozart Quintet in C with Cecil Aronowitz.

Perhaps their most memorable visit to Aldeburgh was outside the Festival when, on 19 December 1976, a bare fortnight after Britten's death, they gave the world première of his third string quartet. The quartet had been written especially for the Amadeus to play, and they had journeyed to Aldeburgh for a couple of days in late September to go over the work with the composer. It was generally known that Britten might not have long to live and it was a matter of great pride and consolation to the Quartet that they were able to learn the piece with the composer, rehearse it with him in his library at the Red House, and then perform the whole work to him. Despite Britten's poor health and the fact that he tired easily, he was mentally at his most acute. As always, his intense musicality was expressed in thoroughly practical and helpful terms. Brainin recalls Britten suggesting details of fingering that helped him to master one particularly intransigent passage; Schidlof remembers how the composer gave him tips on trilling and on how to edge more easily out of a *tremolando* passage in the first movement.

When the complete work seemed at last to be 'under the fingers' and the Amadeus played it through, Britten turned at one point to Donald Mitchell who was present, beamed, and said, 'You know, Donald, it

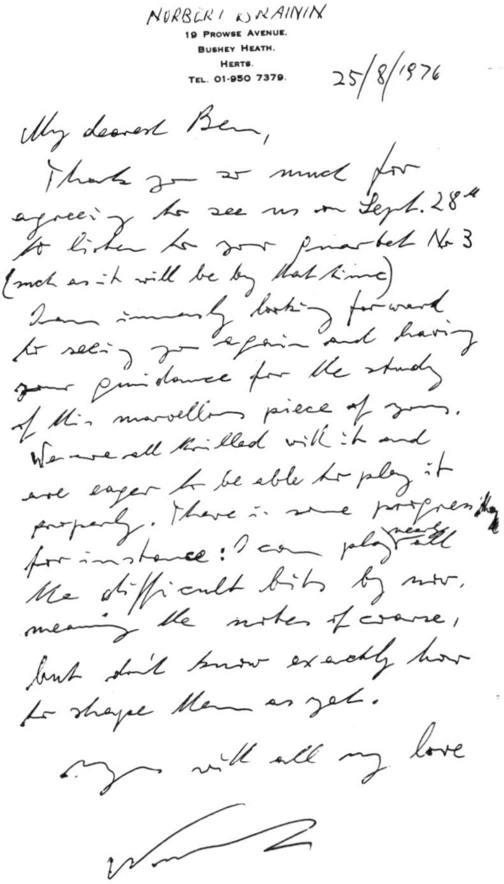
NORBERT BRAININ
19 Prowse Avenue.
Bushey Heath.
Herts.
Tel. 01-950 7379.
25/8/1976
My dearest Ben,
Thank you so much for
agreeing to see us on Sept. 28th
to listen to your Quartet No 3
(such as it will be by that time)
I am immensely looking forward
to seeing you again and having
your guidance for the study
of this marvellous piece of yours.
We are all thrilled with it and
are eager to be able to play it
properly. There is some progress
for instance: I can play nearly all
the difficult bits by now,
meaning the notes of course,
but don't know exactly how
to shape them as yet.
with all my love

Norbert Brainin's letter to Benjamin Britten after rehearsing with him his third string quartet. It reads: Thank you so much for agreeing to see us on Sept 28th to listen to your Quartet no. 3 (such as it will be by that time). I am immensely looking forward to seeing you again and having your guidance for the study of this marvellous piece of yours. We are all thrilled with it and are eager to be able to play it properly. There is some progress, for instance: I can play nearly all the difficult bits by now, meaning the notes of course, but don't know exactly how to shape them as yet. With all my love, Norbert.

works!' The Quartet was due to visit Aldeburgh again in October for further rehearsal with the composer but by then Britten was too weak to see them. On 4 December he died and at the première a couple of weeks later, according to all those present in the audience, the Amadeus Quartet gave an intensely moving account of one of the most important contributions to the string repertoire of modern times.

In addition to Dartington and Aldeburgh, the Amadeus have been regular visitors to the Edinburgh, York, Bath and other British Festivals and have given a regular series of six or eight more or less monthly concerts each season in London. Alone, or in conjunction with other artists, their presence has added distinction to the inauguration of new concert halls (the Queen Elizabeth Hall in 1967 and St. John's, Smith Square two years later) and of new concert series (the first season of European Broadcasting Union concerts in 1967, when they shared the opening concert with Benjamin Britten and Peter Pears). When Edward Heath was Prime Minister, the Amadeus Quartet was invited to perform at 10 Downing Street and at Chequers. Internationally, scarcely a season has gone by since the early 1950s when the Quartet has not appeared in Germany and/or Italy and it has also made increasingly regular visits to Scandinavia, the Netherlands, Belgium, France and other continental countries. Every second year the Amadeus make an extensive tour of the United States, and every five or six they like to re-acquaint themselves with their audiences in New Zealand, Australia, Korea, Japan and elsewhere in the further reaches of the globe. Among their more notable milestones have been performances in the USSR, Hungary, Czechoslovakia, East Germany and elsewhere in the communist world; a tour of Latin America in 1970; and – what was surely a 'first' in several respects – an appearance in Lebanon at the Baalbeck Festival in 1971 immediately prior to one at the Israel Festival. Asked to list the countries in which they have played they tend to reply by trying to list those in which they have *not*.

The facts and figures of the Amadeus story are daunting. No comparable group has had so uninterruptedly distinguished a career or achieved anything like such an accumulation of accolades. Its members have honorary doctorates from the University of York (whose quartet in residence they were for several weeks in 1967 and 1968) and are Honorary Members of the Royal Academy of Music; they have each been given the Order of the British Empire by Queen Elizabeth, and from the Germans they have received the coveted Bundesverdienstkreuz, First Class (Grand Cross of the Order of Merit). On the occasion of their 25th anniversary as a quartet in January 1973, the Amadeus received from Deutsche Grammophon the rare distinction of a *Golden Gramophone* award – an appropriate gesture from a company for whom the Quartet has now sold something approaching two million records. And a year later they were awarded the Austrian Cross of Honour for Services to Art and Science.

The Amadeus Quartet has undoubtedly earned its success. You only get to the top in the competitive world of serious music if you are very good, and you only stay there by continuing to be good. But the long-lasting success of the Amadeus Quartet is also part of a wider musical story. Just as the musical history of the years preceding their Wigmore Hall début had helped to create the ideal circumstances for a new young ensemble to get off to a good start, the musical history of the years that followed also played its part in helping to carry the Quartet along on the crest of a never ebbing wave of success.

During the generation following the end of World War II much of the Western world enjoyed a boom and so did its musical life. And in this musical renaissance, Britain – and London in particular – took pride of place. This musical pre-eminence was all the more impressive because so unexpected. Not that Britain had not occasionally produced and often welcomed musicians of the highest stature. Henry Purcell was a composer of genius; Haydn's visits to London were an important chapter in musical history; Mendelssohn was almost adopted as the official British composer-conductor. Around the turn of the nineteenth and twentieth centuries, the Savoy operas and Elgar's *Gerontius* and *Enigma Variations* ranked with the highest achievements of their respective *genres*, while singers like Mary Garden, Maggie Teyte and Eva Turner were interpreters of international renown. But the triumphs of Britain's musical life often left something to be desired. Many of the great names within Britain were of foreigners who vouchsafed to visit the country and leave behind a little of their inscrutable continental magic while British artists of incontestable talent often had to live and work abroad if they were to carve out for themselves the careers their talents warranted. By the early decades of this century, there was one British artist of world renown who made music in Britain, Sir Thomas Beecham, but he was something of a rogue elephant, the exception that proves the rule. Beecham was forever complaining that managements persisted in engaging foreign artists instead of British ones,

47

forgetting in an uncharacteristic display of either amnesia or modesty that with the exception of himself most British artists were inferior to their non-British counterparts.

After 1945, miraculously, centuries of traditional British second-bestness – or the belief, at least, that this was traditional – were over-turned. Many of the world's musical superstars – Solti, Barenboim, Brendel, Menuhin, Klemperer – were making their permanent homes and giving their most frequent public performances in London. London had five symphony orchestras of international quality where most comparable cities in other countries had no more than one, while some of Britain's provincial orchestras (notably the Hallé under Barbirolli and the Royal Liverpool under John Pritchard and Charles Groves) were capable of attaining the highest standards. At Covent Garden, opera casts were increasingly likely to include names like Joan Carlyle, Amy Shuard or Geraint Evans alongside those of Carlo Bergonzi, Sena Jurinac or Boris Christoff, while any night of the week at the Royal Festival Hall you might have heard (by the later 1960s at least) young British musicians of international calibre like Janet Baker, John Ogdon or Colin Davis and, on occasion, new works by rising composers like Harrison Birtwistle, Alexander Goehr, Peter Maxwell Davies or John Tavener. London was the mecca of serious music, and it was the ambition of every musician of quality to perform or be performed there. Gone were the days when London only accepted a musician after he had made his name elsewhere. By the 1960s London itself was the place above all whose recognition and praise every young musician craved.

In a sense it was just fortuitous that the Amadeus Quartet was formed and based in the city that was fast becoming the musical capital of the world. Certainly the close correlation between the successful history of the Amadeus and the story of London's musical pre-eminence is on the face of it little more than a nice coincidence. However, the two stories do have elements in common for many of the factors that helped to project London into its musical prominence are already familiar from the narrower story we have been chronicling.

The most obvious is the war. Just as the war played a pivotal part in the personal lives of three of the members of the Amadeus Quartet, it was also the most essential element in projecting London to its important position in the musical world in the years that followed. The repercussions of World War II merely on the musical life of Europe would themselves warrant a substantial book, but let us briefly note just three. The first is that the cultural life of central Europe was totally disrupted by the

The Quartet with (above) *Mstislav Rostropovich and* (below) *Frederick Thurston.*

Above: *Max Rostal with colleagues and students* (left to right): *Siegmund Nissel, Alfred Cave, Robert Masters, Kinloch Anderson, Joan Spencer* (front), *Rostal* (centre), *Bernard Stevens* (with glasses, behind Rostal), *Martin Lovett, Leonard Dight, Maria Lidka* (front, next to Rostal), *Peter Schidlof, Muriel Taylor, Norbert Brainin, Yfrah Neaman.* Below: *The Quartet with David Oistrakh and Mrs Charles Berg, the wife of the honorary secretary of the Musica Viva Society, Sydney, 1958.*

Above left: *Joseph Szigeti meets the Nissels' daughter, Claire.* Above right: *Benjamin Britten with Martin and Peter Lovett.* Centre: *Nissel and Lovett with Rostropovich.* Below: *Martin, Sam (father) and Suzanne Rozsa Lovett with Pablo Casals, Prades, 1959.*

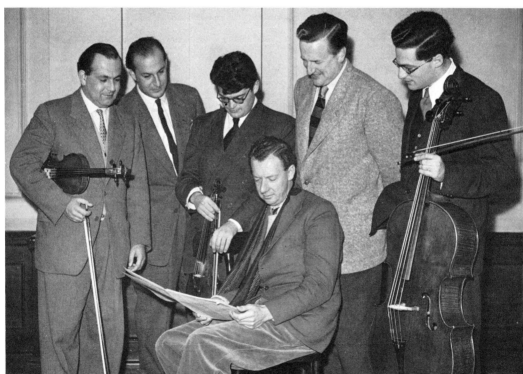

With Benjamin Britten in the USSR (above) *and* (below) *with Britten and Peter Pears.*

traumas of the Third Reich so that many of the most substantial musical figures of Poland, Germany, Austria and Italy were disgraced, dead, in captivity or, if they were lucky, far away from their homeland. What remained in many cities where great music had once been created and performed was all too often block after block of desolate rubble and millions upon millions of hungry, derelict people. For these stark, physical reasons, the old capitals of world music, above all Berlin and Vienna, had inevitably to pass the laurel wreath elsewhere.

But the war had had political as well as material repercussions, one of the most far-reaching of which was that the principal victors, the USA and the USSR, had divided Europe into spheres of influence and interest along a line that went right through the pre-war musical heartland. Almost at the stroke of a pen, people in Warsaw, Berlin and Hamburg, Munich, Prague and Vienna found themselves on the geographical edge of their areas of greatest political, social and economic activity rather than in the middle. Thus, the relegation in cultural importance of the great towns of central Europe that was occasioned by the defeat of Hitler's Reich was extended by the consequent establishment of the Iron Curtain. Berlin's loss, however, was London's gain, in the almost literal sense that many of the central Europeans – particularly Jews – who had been lucky enough to escape the cataclysm that befell their homelands inevitably found themselves after the war in the Western democracies. These countries, while not generous in their attitude towards those from central Europe who had sought asylum, found that those to whom they had given refuge proved to be among the most important cultural leaders of the next generation. Thus the war not only robbed the great cities of central Europe of the cultural pre-eminence some of them had enjoyed before, but it also transplanted many important carriers of middle European culture to places like London and New York. Without the Third Reich, not only would Berlin and Vienna presumably have retained some of their former musical glory, but young musicians like Brainin, Schidlof and Nissel would never have dreamed of studying – much less settling – in London.

There are other factors that link the story of the Amadeus to that of the wider eddies and flows of musical history. One is the BBC. This public corporation had always taken very seriously the responsibilities of public service broadcasting, and never more so than during the war. In the post-war era, it was lucky in having the services of the austere and intellectual Sir William Haley who, as Director General, was largely instrumental in giving the go-ahead for the primarily cultural Third

Programme in 1946. A dozen years later, William Glock – former Schnabel student and *Observer* music critic and since 1953 director of music at the annual Dartington Summer School – became the BBC's Controller of Music, and during the next fourteen years presided with magisterial judgement and the most courageous vision over what had become the biggest patron of serious music in the world.

By the time Glock retired from the BBC in 1972, the Corporation ran a dozen orchestras, broadcast over one hundred hours of serious music (and an average of more than three complete operas) each week on Radio Three alone, was responsible for commissions and performances of much new music and the early exposure of many new artists and, with its Promenade Concerts at London's Royal Albert Hall, ran an annual music festival that reached an aggregate world-wide audience of around 100 million.

But if Glock and the BBC were a mighty factor in helping to steer Britain to musical prominence, they also played an important part in shaping the career of the Amadeus. Glock himself was a great personal friend and colleague, regularly invited the Quartet to his summer schools at Bryanston and Dartington, and often played piano quartets and quintets with them in the early years. In the period of Glock's controllership, the very fact that the BBC put increasing resources into the broadcasting of serious music meant that the name and sound of such a group as the Amadeus Quartet were constantly before a vastly greater public than could ever have been the case in other times or places.

London owed its rise to musical importance to a number of other considerations as well. As America opened itself up in the post-war and Cold War eras to a new and active political, economic and military participation with its European Allies for example, London assumed a geographically central position in the councils of the western world that it had not had in pre-war times.

And as jet planes took over from sea travel in the 1960s, London also became the stop-off or set-off point for people trying to cross the Atlantic cheaply. Much of this applied, of course, to Paris. But France, unlike Britain, had been occupied during the war and had not, therefore, been much of a haven for the refugees from Nazism who were now playing such a substantial part in Britain's musical life. Furthermore, the chronic instability of the Fourth Republic during the years when musical Europe was just getting back on its feet also helped to rule Paris out (until the later 1970s perhaps) from attracting the large and imaginative artistic entrepreneurship for which it had been noted in earlier periods.

The story of why London became the musical capital of the world is long and complex and includes many additional strands. Some are primarily institutional (the Arts Council, the saga of the South Bank concert halls, the new eminence of Britain's colleges of music, the financial attractiveness of London for recording companies) while others would include honorable mention of a great many individual musicians and musical administrators whose combination of faith and action caused music to be where it was not before. For all these reasons and no doubt many more, London became the reigning capital of the post-war musical world and its rise and continued prominence coincided almost exactly with the parallel rise and prominence of one of its most distinguished resident ensembles, the Amadeus Quartet. It is no adverse reflection on the Amadeus to say that its career was aided, particularly in the early years, by the fact that it happened to be based in a nation which was witnessing a veritable explosion of musical activity. Rather, the world-wide success of the Amadeus can be seen as reflecting credit, not only on the outstanding achievements of the Quartet itself, but also on the society and the wider culture that helped foster and develop its powerful talents. The Amadeus Quartet responded to the challenge of being based in an immensely stimulating musical environment and it is, indeed, partly due to them that the international reputation of British music and musicianship was to rise so high in the years ahead.

на 4. V.a   зала **КОНЦЕРТНА ЗАЛА**   начало 19³⁰ ч.

СТРУНЕН КВАРТЕТ

«АМАДЕУС»
ВЕЛИКОБРИТАНИЯ

в състав:

НОРБЕРТ БРАЙНИН
цигулка

ПЕТЕР ШИДЛОФ
виола

ЗИГМУНД НИСЕЛ
цигулка

МАРТИН ЛОВЕТ
виолончело

• в програмата •

ХАЙДН	ШУБЕРТ	БЕТХОВЕН
Квартет оп. 64 № 6	„Квартетзатц" до-минор	Квартет оп. 132

Билети при касата на _____

GETTING IT TOGETHER

'Can you cats play?' And, the man in the American bar might have added, what and how? He would have had a real shock if the members of the Amadeus Quartet had answered his friendly questions in any detail.

Each season the Quartet plays something in the region of sixty works – close to the entire standard quartet repertoire. Few comparable groups maintain so many works at concert pitch. On the other hand, the Amadeus have on occasion been accused of being unadventurous in their choice of repertoire. Of course, say the critics, the backbone of any string quartet must be the great works by Haydn, Mozart, Beethoven, Schubert and Brahms; but shouldn't Debussy, Ravel and perhaps Janacek have a regular outing – to saying nothing of Schoenberg and Webern?

There are several answers. For one thing, the Amadeus do include modern works in their repertoire. They have played not only Bartok, Hindemith, Tippett and Britten but also – particularly in their early years – Priaulx Rainier, Egon Wellesz, Mátyás Seiber, Peter Racine Fricker, Benjamin Frankel and Arwel Hughes. Nonetheless, it does remain broadly true that their repertoire concentrates more heavily on the classics than on modern pieces. The Juilliard Quartet, for instance, or the LaSalle often make a point of including difficult modern works in their programmes, almost as though they felt they had a mission to educate and extend the tastes of their public. Don't the members of the Amadeus have something of the same proselytizing feeling? 'Oh no, there's nothing of the missionary about us!' they laugh.

In part, the relative conservatism of the Amadeus arises out of the sheer mechanics of programming. The Quartet is signed up for most of its concert dates a year or two in advance. Once an engagement has been fixed, it is initially up to the local concert society to propose a programme on the basis of a document containing a list of current offerings plus scheduling guidelines* which the Quartet circulates. The local societies almost invariably ask for the standard classics; even a Bartok or Britten work will, if included in the list, be requested for no more than a handful of the Quartet's hundred or so engagements for the year concerned. Of course, special occasions can require special programmes, and the Quartet is not above laying down the law to a society that puts in a silly proposal. But, generally speaking, the Quartet does tend to try to play what it is asked to play and this, inevitably, is a further pressure in the direction of the standard repertoire. In addition, it is only fair to add that it is this that the Quartet does best. It is outstanding, some would say unmatched, in the Viennese classics; there is a quality of controlled improvisation in its Schubert, for example, that can be breathtaking. But, however hard the Quartet works at Berg's *Lyric Suite* or the Webern op. 28, its performance is unlikely to surpass that of one of an ensemble like the Juilliard that specializes in modern works. There was a time when it devoted more attention to difficult modern works and the players still enjoy – and excel in – the few that they do. But most listeners agree, their style is essentially lyrical, and to the Amadeus the rhythmic and tonal irregularities of Webern or Schoenberg, while technically not unmanageable, feel music- ally somewhat alien.

At one time, the Quartet approached Hans Keller and asked him to help advise them about working on some Schoenberg. He suggested that the fourth quartet was the most appropriate with which to start but recalls that things did not progress very satisfactorily. The problem was not the technical conundrums that Schoenberg posed. On the contrary, says Keller, they got over all these incidental difficulties with great aplomb. But, he adds with a characteristically revealing paradox, the better they played, the worse they played. In other words, the more they got the *notes* right, the more they displayed their basic antipathy to the *music*. The Quartet put a lot of work into their attempts to master Schoenberg and greatly valued Keller's help, but nonetheless returned eventually to the great corpus of works with which they felt musically more at home.

Does this mean that they play safe? Not according to Sir William

*See *The Repertoire* and *Suggested Programmes* pp. 131–135.

54

Glock. He suggests that they gravitate towards music that moves them, music of substance and nobility that will bear endless repetition and re-studying. 'I can't imagine them playing someone like Jean Françaix, for instance, or any music that is trivial, however well written.' On the other hand, Glock adds, 'They probably find the chamber works of a great modern figure like Schoenberg hard to construe and don't, perhaps, get enough pleasure from him soon enough to convince themselves that they really want to persevere with him.'

As for the question of *how* the Amadeus plays, this is something that each listener must decide for himself. Many who are attracted to Amadeus performances say that it is because of the sweep and energy of execution and the smooth clarity and beauty of tone. William Mann, music critic of *The Times*, in his review of the 25th birthday concert in 1973, thought the achievement of the Amadeus could be summed up as 'power, attack, a full yet clean sound, total identification with the music . . . intensity and polished virtuosity . . . nowadays they are not afraid to risk some roughness of tone in the interests of truth and aspiration.'

Many listeners would agree with this view. There are some, however, who take exception to what they regard as a slightly cloying quality occasionally present in the Amadeus approach, an inclination to punctuate rather than understate, a tendency (particularly noticeable with Brainin) to use a wide vibrato*, and feel that the Quartet as a whole is sometimes guilty of infusing yesterday's thoughts and feelings into today's performances. 'The Amadeus Quartet,' wrote the critic Conrad Wilson in *The Scotsman* in 1964, is like Herbert von Karajan – so perfect a musical machine, so smooth, so effortless, so beautifully balanced that people are forever condemning it for its virtues. Its tone, we are nowadays regularly told, is too lovely, its rhythm too glib.'

Much of this is largely a matter of taste. The members of the Amadeus Quartet, like any busy performers, are not invariably at the very peak of their collective form and are no doubt as guilty as any comparable group of occasional Homeric nods. They are aware of the objections that are sometimes made of their playing and acknowledge that, at different periods in their history, they might have been vulnerable to different

*Everything is relative. In August 1971, the music critic of the *Jerusalem Post*, praising an Amadeus performance that had just been given in Tel Aviv as part of the Israel Festival, commented admiringly on Brainin's 'restrained vibrato . . . This is in wonderful contrast to the excessive and often nervous vibrato of most of our own violinists.'

types of legitimate criticism. In particular the foursome tend to acknowledge that in the early years they might have been so concerned about the niceties of precision and tidiness that not enough leeway was left to the sort of inspiration of the moment that can give a performance that extra lift. Most critics tend to agree, however, that during its second and third decades of existence the Quartet increasingly allowed its improvisatory instincts to have greater sway so that more and more matters of overall interpretation (though not the individual technical problems that arose) could be left to the sense of occasion generated by each concert. Although most listeners are astonished at the almost total absence of ragged edges in Amadeus playing and some even criticize the Quartet for this, the players themselves feel that more is left to the mood of the moment now than was once the case and that the accusation of being *too* clean or *too* beautiful, if it was ever justifiable, is no longer so.

Of course, how you play partly depends upon where you are playing, and partly for whom. For instance, there is obviously a difference between a concert and a recording. 'The difference,' said Lovett in an interview published in *Hi Fi News* in April 1973, 'is roughly parallel with the theatre and the cinema. The theatre at its best is far superior to anything that could happen in the cinema, for there are moments in a great theatrical performance which never happen elsewhere. But on the other hand I'd rather go to the cinema than see anything that was less than absolutely first class in the theatre.'

In a recording, as in a film, everything can be controlled – so there is no excuse if any loose edges are left. In the next chapter, we will have a glimpse of the hard work which is necessary for the Amadeus to get the recordings absolutely 'right'. In a recording, every detail has to be right since any audible error will ingrain itself upon the mind of the listener. But even here it is on the overall 'feel' of a performance rather than on technical perfection that the Amadeus Quartet now tends to concentrate.

This is particularly the case with a composer like Beethoven. The Amadeus has played all Beethoven's quartets many times, has performed complete Beethoven cycles in half a dozen of the world's great music capitals, and is re-recording the late quartets twenty years after having committed the entire cycle to disc. Beethoven, they all emphasize, was not only a great creative genius but also a supremely practical musician and an outstanding interpreter. 'What he put down on paper,' says Brainin, 'is his own marvellous interpretation of his own creative ideas.' To Lovett, Beethoven 'was one of us' – a real man of flesh and blood whose titanic conceptions were only put down on paper after the most excruciating effort. 'When I play Beethoven,' he says, 'I get the impression that he knew what it would feel like actually playing the piece, so that the performer is virtually sharing with him an insight into the very process of creation.' That process involves struggle and a certain emotional volatility – and this must be reflected in the way the works are played. The important thing is the mood of the piece, rather than the details. The occasional tonal or dynamic indiscretion is not always unpardonable (at least in a live performance). What *is* unpardonable is an overall interpretation that does not truly communicate the state of mind that Beethoven is trying to project. 'It's as though you're looking at Everest,' Lovett goes on. 'You wouldn't notice, or be worried about, some little cloud that obscured one bit of the gigantic view revealed to you of the whole.'

Do the members of the Amadeus then play incorrect notes? Perhaps they have committed their share from time to time (though it is only fair to add that, in general, their intonational accuracy is one of their most distinguished characteristics). But all four are quick to reiterate the point that this question of the relative importance of technical detail is in part a matter not only of the circumstances in which you are playing but, vitally, which composer.

Mozart, they all agree, is the hardest composer to play well. To get Mozart right, *nothing* – individual notes, dynamics, balance, or overall structure and interpretation – must be incorrect. In Mozart, the emotions are as intense as in Beethoven and yet as stylized as in Haydn. Playing Mozart is like walking a tightrope, say the Amadeus; you've *got* to do exactly what he says or you'll fall off on one side or another. 'Unlike Beethoven,' says one player, 'it's hard to feel that Mozart was one of us, struggling away against the limitations of the human condition.' With Mozart (and perhaps with Schubert) you are in another sphere. 'If a Mozart piece goes well,' says another, 'you almost feel you're in a state of grace.'*

So: how do the members of the Amadeus play? The answer must be that they play – or at any rate, approach – different composers differently. Their Beethoven is not like their Mozart or their Schubert and it is right that it is not. All four are, fundamentally, instinctive players not primarily given to scholarly analysis during the hurry and bustle of a busy life, and they themselves are largely at a loss to explain their interpretative

*The experience of performing Mozart well can evoke from sensitive musicians the most unexpected metaphors. Elisabeth Söderström describes singing Mozart under a really good conductor as 'akin to perfect sexual harmony'.

approaches to this or that composer or work in more than the most general or even metaphysical terms (except, of course, in their role as teachers where a more analytical approach is essential). The sort of musical insights which normally inform their playing are not unlike those of a first class actor who, while feeling ill at ease if asked to *explain* his interpretation of *Hamlet*, nevertheless gives his audience unmistakable evidence of having familiarized himself with the underlying meaning of every word he utters and of having grasped, and learned how to communicate, the overall inter-relationships that exist between the various elements of the play. Ask a member of the Amadeus why he accentuates this or that note and he will probably throw the question back and ask why you say 'To *be* or *not* to be' rather than stressing the word 'or'. 'At some point you have to realize the emotional and realistic content of *every* bar,' one of them emphasizes. 'Once you've experienced this, you're unlikely to make any really serious errors because from that point on you're able to read the whole score just as the composer wrote it.'

Some listeners have commented, often but not invariably with approval, on a certain 'Viennese' style that they feel the Amadeus Quartet embodies. What do the foursome think? First reactions tend to be unprintable. 'Most people in Vienna are at least as unmusical as most people anywhere else' would be a mild and very loose paraphrase. But on reconsideration they are prepared to acknowledge that there may be something to this sort of label. Brainin quotes a Viennese saying to the effect that the greatest songs are those that are never written ('Heard melodies are sweet, but those unheard/Are sweeter' – it is Lovett quoting Keats) and suggests that the greatest music of the classical period in Vienna was characterized by its capacity to communicate by means of understatement. He sings the lilting opening to the *cavatina* from Beethoven's op. 130, which is marked *sotto voce*. (A)

The mood of this music is deeply introspective, says Brainin, and it should be played with the utmost restraint. Restraint of utterance as a response to a surfeit of feeling – this is how Brainin characterizes the tradition of Viennese music and Viennese music-making at its greatest, and this, he acknowledges, is a quality the Amadeus Quartet tries to embody.

Schidlof agrees, and cites the *scherzo* of Schubert's A minor Quartet. This requires a lilt, an almost imperceptible holding back, a capacity to let the music make its own point while not playing it in a wooden manner. 'Maximum communication by minimum means' is how he puts it. Minimum means? The Amadeus Quartet has sometimes been accused of

(A) **Cavatina.**
Adagio molto espressivo

having too small a tone. But sheer volume, all its members insist, is no virtue (and they tend to quote the 'noisy' or 'aggressive' accounts of this or that work that they have occasionally heard from certain American ensembles). If there is an overall stylistic (as opposed to technical) virtue that the Amadeus Quartet admires, it is the capacity to communicate by introspection and implication where necessary rather than to aim at achieving impact merely by power. And this, they concede, might be given the sobriquet 'Viennese'.

These questions are, however, hopelessly intangible. The critics contradict each other and seem to hear opposite qualities in the same performances. Musicians themselves – certainly this is true of the Amadeus Quartet – are often at a loss to define or even describe the qualities of their own music-making. The very nature of music tends to preclude easy verbal description. The story is told of Schumann (and no doubt others; it could easily have originated with Brahms) that when asked by a gushing fan how he composed he answered to the effect that he got up in the morning, had his breakfast, sat down at his desk, picked up his pen, scratched his head for a minute or two, and then started to write down notes. Ask the members of the Amadeus Quartet how they play, and you might get a similar reply. Are they more forthcoming when asked how they feel their own interpretations differ from those of other Quartets? One Amadeus member admires the chording of the Quartetto Italiano while another acknowledges the rhythmic vitality of the Juilliard. But ask them how their own *Hunt* or *Dissonance* or *Aus Meinem Leben* differs from that of one of their rivals and they either point to a phrase here or a nuance there that, for reasons that are hard to explain, 'we' do it this way and 'they' do that, or else they resort to general phrases about structural integrity and being true to what they consider to have been the composer's intentions. Interpretative opinions and instincts simply vary, even among artists universally acknowledged to be of the highest level of technical mastery.

But what is it about Amadeus interpretations that many love and some criticize? To many of the Amadeus's most devoted listeners (and to their critics, too), the unique quality of Amadeus performances is to an important degree generated by the musical personality of Norbert Brainin. This is entirely understandable for no quartet could flourish with an identifiable musical personality of its own unless its first violinist had a powerful and coherent conception of the works it undertook. The first violin must be *primus* even if the other three are still *pares*, for it is the first violin that is most often given the most conspicuous and charac-teristic passages, the first statement of a major theme, the opportunity to suggest and mould the character of an entire work.

The early history of the genre goes back to the late seventeenth and early eighteenth centuries, when composers wrote little *divertimenti* for solo violin and string accompaniment. Under the refinements of Haydn and Mozart, this form became extended and, eventually, developed into the string quartet. If the concerto (which was taking shape at about the same time) gave ever greater emphasis to the role of the soloist, the quartet gradually *reduced* the independent role of the soloist and upgraded those of the other instruments. In the greatest quartets, particularly those of the later classical period, each of the four instruments plays an increasingly independent role while contributing equally to the overall musical composition. In his last quartet, op. 135, Beethoven actually splits a single phrase between all four instruments (something that Bartok was to do a century later throughout his quartet writing). Some of the major works for the genre are thus no longer merely solo displays with accompaniment but genuine, integrated works for four instruments; and a similar development occurred – a century or more later – in the corporate personality of the groups that played them.

In the late nineteenth century, it was still possible for a virtuoso violinist like Joachim to travel from city to city playing quartets at each stop with a locally recruited threesome; each group would be known as the 'Joachim Quartet' and it is even reported that the great man would stand as the others sat. In the twentieth century, the tradition continued of a quartet being named after its leader, almost always the first violinist, though by now the dominance of a figure like Adolf Busch was no more than a fair statement of the personality whose musicianship gave the ensemble its distinctive character.

In time, however, everything took on an increasingly democratic mien and it became fashionable for quartets to give themselves non-personal names. In keeping with such a climate of opinion, the Amadeus Quartet decided not to name itself after its leader and, in general, to be as democratic as possible. That is, all four members of the Quartet have always expressed their view about all matters, musical or otherwise, and, indeed, they each hope and expect to be scrutinized and criticized by all three of their colleagues. Discerning listeners have always emphasized that the outstanding characteristic of the Amadeus Quartet is the way in which four players, each with his own independent musical personality and his own distinctive gifts to bring, manage to combine these various gifts in the interests of the communal exercise in which they are all engaged so that the whole transcends the sum of its not inconsiderable parts. Indeed, it is this communality of endeavour that gives the Quartet its special stamp. Take away any one of the four contributing parts and substitute another, and the entire voice would be altered. In a way this is a purely hypothetical matter as there have never been any substitutes and never will be. But there is one striking piece of evidence. For close on thirty years the Amadeus Quartet almost always played the viola quintets with Cecil Aronowitz as second viola – indeed, Aronowitz more or less became an honorary member of the Quartet. After his untimely death in 1978, the Quartet could not at first bring itself to play those works with anybody else. But when it eventually did, in 1980, people who heard the performances said the whole sound was entirely different.

In two respects, both musical, the Amadeus Quartet is not entirely democratic. In the first place – and this becomes clear to anyone who watches the Quartet at rehearsal – all matters of taste and interpretation have to be agreed upon unanimously. If three members like a particular nuance or method of bowing or phrasing and the fourth does not, they will all without demur agree to work on the alternative approaches until all four are in absolute accord. 'There is no place for compromise or for a majority opinion in a good string quartet,' says Brainin with finality. Which brings us to the second respect in which the Amadeus Quartet is not entirely democratic.

There are some quartets which claim to have no leader, and the quartet repertoire is sufficiently varied to require each instrument to take the musical lead from time to time. But many listeners and critics nonetheless point to the leadership of Norbert Brainin as one of the qualities that has helped the Amadeus Quartet to carve its unique niche in musical history. While Brainin's leadership may occasionally seem to be reinforced by a volatile and expressive temperament, it is also founded upon the solid rock of outstanding musicianship. 'There is a spiritual quality about his music-making,' wrote John Amis a few years ago, 'a breadth of conception that greatly helps to set this quartet apart from the others, certainly in the works of the great classical composers. He has a way of spinning a phrase, articulating a rhythm and sensing *tempo* nuances which give life to the music he is playing; but, marvellous as the details are, they are always subservient to the conception of the movement as a whole or, indeed, the entire work.'

Brainin's musical intelligence is not that of the analytical academic scholar, and he will often assert himself on some point of balance or intonation or even of repertoire in terms which the others may consider intemperate. But when any of the others has a musical point to make, he is likely to bounce it off Brainin first as though his favourable reaction would confer extra validity. This is, of course, sensitive and touchy territory, and the casual observer might easily be misled by Brainin's occasionally explosive manner (or, for that matter, by Nissel's quiet diplomacy) into believing that personal styles of expression are accurate and adequate representations of musical insight. They are not. Nissel is relatively quiet and diplomatic at rehearsal but a vociferous stickler when it comes to any matter that he considers worth fighting for; Brainin can all too easily order someone to rectify an error for which he was himself responsible. But for all this his presence has undoubtedly added a special distinctiveness to the achievement of the Amadeus Quartet.

Leadership is an elusive and intangible matter. Leadership of some sort virtually always develops whenever a group of people regularly meets to deliberate together, and in a string quartet it is almost bound to inhere to some extent in the first violinist, the person most often called upon to play the most beautiful, the most difficult, or simply the most immediately distinguishable passages in a work. Even in the most subtly integrated works, it is the first violin part that often impresses itself first upon the attention and memory of the listener. But does it follow that the style and quality of an entire ensemble are necessarily derived from those of the first violinist? Or that by virtue of the part he plays he is thereby more likely than his three colleagues to influence the musical personality of the group as a whole?

The experience of various quartets does not suggest a precise answer to these questions. The Aeolian changed its leader in 1970; the Juilliard has changed everybody except its leader over the years; the Guarneri is said to have no leader – and, as if to emphasize the point, the Guarneri second violin, John Dalley, rather than the first violinist, Arnold Stein-hardt, often plays in the works, piano and flute quartets and the like, that require only one violin. From where, or from whom, do the present day Aeolian, Juilliard, or Guarneri derive their characteristic musical person-ality, or, as one might say, take their lead? In the case of the Juilliard, the presence of Robert Mann has given the ensemble a continuity of style over the years that has to some extent survived changes of personnel, though the arrival of a brilliant and powerful figure like Emanuel Hurwitz to lead the Aeolian must have contributed to a certain sense of *dis*continuity. There are quartets that have changed personnel and direction so radically over the years that there is little continuous except the name ('Rather like a football team,' snorts Norbert Brainin). The Guarneri have remained unchanged since they were formed in 1965 so that, if there were any apparent rudderlessness that critics might want to attribute to the lack of a 'leader', it would be more than offset by the sense of unity and purpose that are manifestly shared by the four founder members after a decade and a half of playing together.

What all this boils down to is that the style and quality of a quartet can clearly stand to benefit a great deal from the musical personality of its first violinist. If he is a larger-than-life character like Norbert Brainin, and if his talents are mediated by the utter reliability and sensitivity of Siegmund Nissel and his invariable capacity totally to attune his own string tone to the requirements of overall balance, and by the mellow richness and dynamic impulse of Schidlof and Lovett, then the basic ingredients are there for an ensemble of quite outstanding quality. If the same four people, with the same subtle interweaving of their individual talents, continue to live and grow together over the span of an entire working lifetime, the result is likely to attain a consistent standard of excellence rarely matched in the history of the art.

How far can the quality of the 'Amadeus sound' be attributed to the instruments the Quartet play? Peter Schidlof, Siegmund Nissel and Martin Lovett each play a Stradivarius while Norbert Brainin usually performs on a Guarneri del Gesu. Each of the instruments is an outstanding work of art combining great delicacy and sensitivity of tone with superb projection. Brainin's 1734 Guarneri del Gesu, which he bought in the early 1970s, once belonged to the great French violinist, Jacques Pierre Joseph Rode, and was used by Rode when he gave the first performance of Beethoven's G minor Sonata op. 96 in the presence of the composer. Possibly the most distinguished of the Amadeus instruments is Schidlof's 1701 'Macdonald' Strad. In a letter to the Rudolph Wurlitzer Company of New York in 1926, Alfred Hill, one of the directors of the distinguished London firm of dealers and co-author of the authoritative study of Stradivari, says: 'I have seen every existing specimen and, judged as a whole, I place this viola at the top.' Schidlof is justifiably proud of the compact yet expressive tone of his Strad. The bigger, more voluptuous-toned Brescian instruments can sometimes spread too much, he feels, and can occasionally need to be 'forced' if they are to get through to the audience across the wall of violins and cello. But with his Macdonald Strad he feels he has 'the Rolls-Royce of instruments' and is able to project a clear, unforced tone that can be heard in the back row of the largest halls – particularly, he is quick to add, halls with the acoustical sensitivity of La Scala, Milan or Berlin's Philharmonic Hall.

Each of the four players speaks with glowing pride about his instrument and treats it with the utmost reverence. But the quality of an instrument is not the fundamental ingredient of good playing. Indeed, each of the four players stresses that, while the early eighteenth century Cremona antiques on which they perform are magnificent to play on, a good player can obtain an almost equally beautiful sound from a less expensive instrument – though with greater effort – while an inferior player would not be greatly helped by owning one. Tests have been done

Werner Neumeister

Recording with Emil Gilels in Munich, 1971 (see p. 91).

Associated Press

The world tour, 1958: (above) *arriving in Hawaii,* (below) *in Japan.*

Records and Recording

In Baalbeck, Lebanon, 1971.

The Carl Flesch Centenary concert, 1973. Conductor: Yehudi Menuhin. Soloists (left to right): *Ida Haendel, Henryk Szerying, Bronislav Gimpel, Max Rostal. Orchestra includes* (left to right): *Alan Loveday* (top left), *Norbert Brainin, Yfrah Neaman, Siegmund Nissel* (obscured by Szerying), *Suzanne Rozsa Lovett* (in check suit), *Robert Masters* (next to Suzanne Rozsa), *Peter Schidlof, Nannie Jamieson* (viola), *Joan Dickson and Martin Lovett* (cello).

The jury for the Carl Flesch prize, 1974. Left to right: (seated) *Max Rostal, Yehudi Menuhin, Wolfgang Schneiderhan, Lennox Berkeley;* (standing) *Norbert Brainin, Ion Voicu, Theo Olof, Nikita Magaloff, Yfrah Neaman.*

The Rudolph Wurlitzer Co.
Dealers in Rare Old Violins
FOUNDED IN 1856
By RUDOLPH WURLITZER
120 WEST 42nd STREET, NEW YORK

CINCINNATI
CHICAGO

CLEVELAND
SAN FRANCISCO

Rare Old Violin Department
New York

Antonius Stradivarius 1704
The "Betts"

Certificate No. *5242*

New York, *November 23rd* 1926

We certify that the *Viola* sold by us to *Mr. Felix M. Warburg* of *New York, N. Y.*

was made by *the celebrated Master, Antonio Stradivari, in Cremona in the year 1701 as indicated by its original label &c.*

Description *The back is formed by one piece of handsome curly maple with a broadish figure which extends upward from left to right across its breadth; the shoulder button is original. The sides are of maple, quarter cut, and match the back. The front is of spruce of medium width of grain of finest quality. The scroll is original and in the Master's finest style. The varnish is original, unusually rich and plentiful, and the color is a beautiful orange-red. The instrument is in an exceptionally fine state of preservation and is known as the "Lord MacDonald," — see pages 101 & 265 of Messrs. Hill's "Life of Stradivari" where it is fully described.*

Measurements:
Length *16 3/16 inches (full)*
Width U. B. *7 5/16 "*
Width L. B. *9 9/16 "*
Width M. B. *5 1/8 "*

5568

Photographs attached.
Hill's Certificate & history attached.

The Rudolph Wurlitzer Co.

by C. Krenz

The certificate of Schidlof's Strad.

to assess whether experts can clearly distinguish the sound of the greatest Italian instruments from good models of a later vintage, and they very rarely can. Nonetheless, the highest standards of playing can only be enhanced further if applied to instruments of the highest standards of craftsmanship: if bad workmen blame their tools, good players like the members of the Amadeus Quartet venerate their instruments.

In much of what the Amadeus Quartet takes on, the stakes are high, and this is as true of the instruments they play as it is of the tough schedule they set themselves. If an inferior instrument gets lost or broken, it can be replaced. Not so a Strad or Guarnerius. The instruments that the Amadeus use are literally irreplaceable but they still have to be insured for huge and somewhat arbitrary sums. And instruments of that calibre have a sensitivity that can verge on the temperamental. Once in North America, when the Amadeus passed in a few hours from 76°F to fourteen inches of snow, Lovett's cello became unglued and had to be put together by a local carpenter. In a humid climate (or hall) the tone quality can deteriorate rapidly and necessitate constant re-tuning. Exposure to draughts can have the same effect. Much worse, however, is an atmosphere that is too dry, for this can cause cracks to develop in the wood. 'If you find yourself in a hotel room with all the radiators up high,' says Nissel, 'the first thing you have to do – and it makes the room pretty uncomfortable – is to run a scalding hot bath so that the fiddle can absorb some of the humidity.'

The world of antique instruments is as full of esoteric hazards (and the occasional crook) as that of antique jewellery. Each of the members of the Quartet can recount a sad story or two of an overpriced – or even fake – instrument or bow that someone almost bought or of a bargain that turned out to be an albatross. And there are also stories about the way in which this or that instrument almost got lost, sat upon, stolen, or forgotten in the helter-skelter of a busy travelling schedule. Lovett once undertook to return all the Amadeus instruments to the group's hotel after a concert in Paris, and arrived at the hotel to discover to his horror that he had left Schidlof's viola on a seat outside the Champs Elysées café where they had all been having a celebratory drink. Fortunately, and amazingly, it was still there when Lovett returned for it an hour later.

The members of the Quartet always carry their own instruments with them on their travels. Lovett used to try to emulate his colleagues and smuggle his cello on to planes as hand luggage (with a little help from his friends who would chat to the stewardesses as he made his furtive way through the various hoops). Nowadays, after years of awkward explanations, he finds it easier to buy it an extra seat. There he sits, fifty or sixty times a year, with a plump, inanimate, unbending Henry Moore lady by his side, as he flies from one engagement to the next.

As for Norbert Brainin's relationship with his instrument, everybody who knew him in the early days has an affectionate story or two of his absent-mindedness. On one occasion during the war he was found to be in a cinema, with his fiddle, when he was supposed to be rehearsing a violin concerto. Then there was the time when the Amadeus Quartet walked onto the concert platform at the Beaux Arts in Brussels, bowed, took their seats – and were then held up as Norbert stood up again, scratched his head, and sensed that something was wrong but wasn't sure what. Then he realized, bounced off to his dressing-room, and reappeared moments later, this time with his violin.

Most of the works the Amadeus Quartet perform were expected to be played in private houses not huge modern concert halls. When Haydn and Mozart played in string quartets the four instrumentalists faced (and played primarily to) each other, even if there happened to be a small, informal audience present. With the advent of the modern concert hall came the problem of projecting these works to audiences of a thousand or more, and with the problem of projection came the problem of how the players were to seat themselves. Many of the world's leading quartets, including all the leading American ensembles, sit in the traditional formation: violin, violin, cello, viola. The Amadeus, like many European quartets, prefers to put the cello on the far side of the viola. There is a certain logic, the members argue, in placing the instruments from left to right in the order of their respective registers from top to bottom, and there is a visual tidiness in seeing a corresponding development from the smaller instruments towards the largest. On the other hand, it also has to be admitted that the cello often has the most distinctive and unmistakable voice in a quartet and regularly provides the underpinning for the whole harmonic structure – an argument for placing it more centrally.

The debate about seating is not confined to string quartets, for orchestras, too, are seated according to variable styles. Most conductors nowadays prefer their strings to be seated clockwise from first fiddles through seconds and violas, to cellos – with double-basses positioned further back either in the middle or on the far right; but some (of whom Sir Adrian Boult was the most notable modern exponent but whose ranks have included Barenboim and Maazel), anxious to bring out certain alternating sonorities, will put the second violins on the right, close to the audience, where the cellos are usually placed. Few modern string quartets have adopted the Boult position and put the second violin on the far right, though this was not uncommon in the nineteenth century and it would be interesting to hear the effect that such a seating pattern would produce. But the respective positioning of the viola and cellos is a matter of earnest debate among today's quartet players and can give rise to the most heated arguments about the nuances of aural and visual symmetry.

To the Amadeus, it is not so much a question of symmetry as of audibility. Brainin emphasizes that it is essential for the first violinist to hear the cello as clearly as possible as these two instruments tend to give the basic structure to much chamber music. Thus, independently of what the audience might think it wants to hear, he insists that the cello should be directly across from him, playing as it were *to* the first violin. As for the other two instruments, the second violin and the viola, these are normally the hardest for ordinary listeners to distinguish because their tonal range is often covered by the first violin above them and the cello below, while the viola in addition has a more mellow tone quality than the three other instruments. Thus, even when the viola part is clearly separated from those of its colleagues, and even when it is playing a solo passage, its voice does not always carry as clearly as it might. When the viola is placed on the edge of the platform opposite the first violin, it is true that it is nearer to the audience. But does the audience hear it better? 'On the contrary,' argues Schidlof, 'the *f*-holes are then projecting the sound away from the audience towards a spot at the back of the stage.' For these reasons, say the members of the Amadeus, it is essential that the second violin and viola – *particularly* the viola – should sit in the middle directly facing the audience.

There are other factors that play a part in helping to determine the particular quality of Amadeus playing and every chamber musician, certainly every Amadeus fan, will have his or her own litany to add to those matters mentioned above. In the end, however, it is hard not to be reduced, as the members of the Quartet themselves are reduced, to a consideration of either the most elusively metaphysical qualities (their ability to 'communicate the composer's intentions' for instance, or to imbue the music with that much-vaunted Viennese style) or else of such relative banalities as their seating plan. Different listeners hear different things, one man's 'delicacy of timbre' is another man's 'schmaltziness' and what one critic hails as 'vigour' another may condemn as 'over-statement'. The members of the Amadeus Quartet are accustomed to the inconsistency with which people hear them, know that the overwhelming public and critical reaction has always been favourable, and take wry comfort from the fact that most critical brick-bats have been tossed back at the heads of those who hurled them by the equal and opposite praise which the same performances have often elicited.

It is only right and proper that the Quartet should be judged by its performances, live and recorded, and it has no reason to feel aggrieved about the public and critical reception that its playing has almost always been given. But in order to reach and sustain the high quality of its playing over the years, a lot of exhausting work has had to be done. The processes of learning, rehearsing, re-rehearsing and polishing are unending, and it is in this relentless pursuit of the highest standards that the collective musical personality of the Amadeus Quartet has repeatedly been forged and tempered anew. Everything is tried out at rehearsal, every tendency allowed its head until, in the end, a more moderate, balanced, consistent collective musical voice is adopted. How does the Amadeus play? Some new answers, and some misleading clues, can be garnered by watching the Quartet at work, behind the scenes.

PLAY IT AGAIN . . .

'Your F sounds rather flat.'

'Why do I have a *sforzando* when nobody else does?'

'Shouldn't we do that passage louder to highlight the *subito piano*?'

The sort of things the members of the Amadeus Quartet say to one another at rehearsals nowadays. Any fundamental musical or personal differences or disagreements, if they ever existed, were ironed out long ago. By now, rehearsals tend to be brisk, intensely professional, and largely wordless.

On this particular morning, in September 1979, things are even brisker than usual and possibly more polite. The pianist Walter Klien has joined Brainin, Schidlof and Lovett at Brainin's house in Bushey Heath, with its breathtaking back window view of the Hertfordshire hills, to rehearse the two Mozart piano quartets for a Queen Elizabeth Hall concert the following day. The Quartet have never worked with Klien before and all present hope that everything will slot into place with a minimum of fuss or bother. The Amadeus players are tired. The night before they had an all Schubert concert in Windsor Castle followed by a reception and dinner – and bed at about 2.30 a.m. Lovett's right shoulder aches this morning and, partly out of jocularity but partly because bowing is painful, he pretends to tune his cello by playing left-handed. Everyone's mood is pleasant, businesslike, and slightly guarded.

'Let's start with the G minor,' Brainin suggests, and the foursome plunge boldly into the opening bar and a half of *allegro* unison playing (A) – and all hit the right *tempo*, timbre and dynamic together.

Klien is obviously well attuned to the Amadeus style, and quickly

71

(A)

establishes his own mastery of the piano part. They play on for a while'
Brainin reminds everyone to take the repeat as it approaches, and the
opening section is more confident the second time around. At the end of
the first movement, a subdued cacophony breaks out. Schidlof retunes his
viola with the help of an A from Klien at the piano, Lovett plays over a
little rhythmical passage that didn't quite click, while the irrepressible
Brainin stands over Klien's shoulder and *ad libs* a cascading piano passage
on his violin while asking the pianist in German whether he thinks the
dynamic balance was quite right at the passage in question.

Quickly the four settle back. Klien launches into the stately *andante*
movement (B) and asks, while playing, whether he has got things right.

'Ja, ja; fine; just right,' the other three tell him and take up the opening
theme as the piano repeats it. They play through the piece with perhaps
eight or ten further interruptions as one or another member of the group

questions some small detail – usually a matter of balance, once or twice something about thythm or intonation. Then a break. Brainin changes a string; he's worried that his tone might be slightly too cutting, too metallic for the Elizabeth Hall. Mrs Brainin brings in coffee. Someone mentions Klemperer and a spate of stories follows. These get bawdier and the imitations funnier when, suddenly, Mrs Brainin looks in again, this time to tell Schidlof that he's wanted on the phone. It's Germany on the line. It seems there's some hitch with the air tickets for Monday. Schidlof, who looks after the group's travel arrangements, spends the next ten minutes phoning Lufthansa, British Airways and sundry travel agents, while the chit-chat among the others – a stretch in English, a stretch in German – switches from Klemperer stories to Royal Family stories. From the Royal Family to Wales. Brainin tells of a Welsh music society that once asked the Amadeus to play whatever it liked 'so long as the programme lasts at least three hours'. Lovett leaps to the rescue of the Welsh by complimenting the unsophisticated audiences of the mining villages to whom they once played on an Arts Council tour. 'Those miners had probably never heard chamber music in their lives,' he says, 'but their instinctive musicianship equipped them to appreciate its cadences, its lyricism, its expressiveness better than many of the richer audiences we tend to get nowadays.'

It's Lovett, his shoulder still aching, who shows the first signs of restlessness. 'Shall we, sort of – well, continue?' he offers to the air. The others fall in with this suggestion, and there follows a lovely, fresh and largely uninterrupted performance of Mozart's other and far sunnier piano quartet, the E flat, K 493.

'Not, of course, a typical Amadeus rehearsal,' Lovett comments as he gets into his new Saab and drives back towards Hampstead. No rehearsal is ever typical, but it is certainly true that this one went extraordinarily smoothly.

Sometimes, particularly when it's just the four 'boys' making music, things aren't quite so polite and the gloves come off a little. It is partly a question of what is at stake: a particularly difficult or relatively unfamiliar work requires uninhibited probing and digging, especially if a recording session or a taxing concert schedule is imminent.

The Verdi quartet is not an easy work to play. There are technical problems that might easily be absorbed within the relative fuzziness of orchestral texture (for which Verdi was accustomed to compose) but

74

which require the utmost accuracy if performed by a quartet. Awkward questions arise, too, about interpretation: what does Verdi mean by his dynamic markings? Unruly nineteenth-century opera singers no doubt needed to be told to go *ppp* if they were not to bawl their heads off in supposedly subdued passages; but does Verdi really want sensitive string players to alternate between the extremes of loudness and softness he specifies? The members of the Amadeus Quartet are no strangers to the Verdi quartet. Indeed, they played it at their professional début at the Wigmore Hall back in 1948 and received glowing reports for their performance. Now, nearly thirty-two years later, they are about to record it and in order to get it absolutely right they pick it apart, almost note for note.

They have a lot on their plate at the moment. In a few days' time they have a concert at the Royal Festival Hall with Stephen Bishop-Kovacevich and have scheduled several sessions with him to rehearse the Brahms F minor Quintet. But as soon as the Brahms concert is over they go off to Munich to record the Verdi (plus the Tchaikovsky Quartet op. 11) so it

(A)

75

is to this difficult work that they must devote much of their available time.

It is 8.30 in the morning in mid-October. Yesterday there were news stories about a possible rail strike and special mid-town parking concessions, so everyone has his car on the road today. The London traffic is appalling as Brainin and Schidlof crawl their way slowly into town towards Nissel's home which backs on to Golders Hill Park and Hampstead Heath in London. They have agreed to a nine o'clock start since Brainin has to get away to a pre-lunch appointment with his Portland Place dentist. Promptly at nine, Siegmund Nissel, a little bleary-eyed and still munching his bowl of muesli, opens the door as the other three arrive within moments of each other. A couple of minutes at the most are devoted to pleasantries. 'Shall we start with the slow movement?' Lovett suggests. 'Yes, the slow movement,' Brainin agrees – and within a split second they're playing. 'There is not another group,' wrote an interviewer in the *Guardian* in 1968, 'which can move into gear like that, with such total involvement and complete rapport, at a nod from any one of the players. It is an Amadeus hallmark and it has taken twenty years to achieve it.' After thirty-two years, this instant rapport happens at such lightning speed that it can not be seen but only believed.

The movement opens with a strange, halting, plaintive tune, yet marked 'with elegance' (A).

They play thirty bars or so. There is some discussion, interspersed with scrutiny of the complete score, about what is presumably intended to be a C flat in the first violin part but against which no accidental is marked. Lovett has some quiet octave jumps in the cello part and seems to recall that, his printed part notwithstanding, they should be played *pizzicato*. Again, a quick glance at the score, and his memory is proved to be correct. Undercurrents of growling are heard as somebody accuses somebody else of being 'hopelessly flat'. A few minutes later, Brainin throws his head back and announces that the rest are playing too loudly – but the other three promptly turn the tables on him and say that they *have* to if they are to have any hope of being heard!

Sparks begin to fly in the next movement. It is a *prestissimo* that opens (B) with a series of brilliant descending phrases for the first violin, somewhat reminiscent of Verdi's 'Spanish' music (Preziosilla's music in *Forza*, for example, or the opening bars of the 'Song of the Veil' scene in *Don Carlos*) and it goes on to include, first, (C) a staccato passage not unlike the gossip music in Act II of *Falstaff*, and then (D) a *cantabile* 'aria' for the cello with an um-pom-pom *pizzicato* accompaniment by the other three. For the listener fine, accessible music – but not easy to play really well. One passage, very fast and very quiet, begins with the first violin alone, and Brainin is again accused of playing too loud (E).

'But it simply can't be played any softer at that speed,' he lectures his colleagues – but proceeds to repeat the passage in question not only softer but also faster with a brilliance that somewhat softens the lash of his tongue. A dashing unison section follows full of unexpected sharps and flats, and the foursome go through this at quarter speed, everyone listening with the utmost care to his own intonation and to that of the others. 'You've got that F wrong six times today,' blurts Schidlof, but his victim accepts the criticism, works at it, gets it right, and listens to everybody else's playing all the more intensively. Lovett wants to do his cello 'aria' once more. It's his tune and he wants to make sure that the other three are accompanying him to his satisfaction. Brainin tries the *pizzicato* accompaniment in various positions on the violin neck. Lovett

(B)

(C)

(D)

(E)

likes the more vibrant sound when the longer strings are plucked – and left 'open' as often as possible. The others agree. They play this section through once more, then do the brilliant *da capo* with Brainin's Spanish-style trills, and the movement comes to an end.

From the kitchen comes the musical hum of Nissel's kettle. Nissel goes off to pour tea and asks Brainin to change his A string for him (which is done with the dexterity with which most people would change a shoe-lace). During the break, Schidlof phones the continent to check next week's hotel bookings, while Lovett calls Ibbs and Tillett about some tickets for Sunday's concert and also discusses with them the idea of re-drafting the regular Amadeus publicity material. Nissel has a complimentary word or two to say about the young man they are about to employ as a business manager. No time today for Klemperer anecdotes or bawdy stories – and it's back to work within about seven minutes. 'I remember having exactly the same problems with this piece when we played it thirty years ago,' says someone ruefully as they re-tune.

(F)

IV. Scherzo Fuga

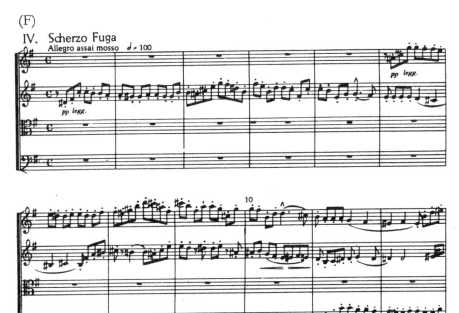

80

Above: *The Amadeus after their honorary degree ceremony at the University of York, 1968.* Below: *Nissel, Schidlof and Lovett join Brainin as recipients of the Order of the British Empire, Buckingham Palace, 1970.*

Jeremy Fletcher

*The Amadeus Quartet being presented with the German Federal Republic's Grand
Cross of the Order of Merit by His Excellency, the West German Ambassador, Karl
Günther von Hase, at a reception held in London at the German Embassy on 13 June 1973.*

Jeremy Fletcher

Jeremy Fletcher

The Amadeus (above) at their Silver Jubilee concert, Queen Elizabeth Hall, January 1973, in front of their earliest poster and (below) with Edward Heath at the post-concert party.

Above (left to right): *Katinka and Norbert Brainin, Sonia and Peter Lovett, Margit and Anne-Marie Schidlof, Siegmund Nissel, Suzanne and Martin Lovett, Daniel Nissel, Peter Schidlof.* Below: *The Brainins, Nissels, Lovetts and Schidlofs together.*

The final movement of the Verdi quartet is a chattering fugue like the one that brings to such a bubbling conclusion his final opera, *Falstaff*. It is an eruption of good spirits – Verdi wrote the quartet as a diversion when some *Aida* rehearsals had to be delayed – but parts of this finale are fiendishly difficult to play accurately. The fugue begins, as do so many, with the second violin (F).

It must be light but energetic, quiet but nimble, and Nissel sets just the right tone and *tempo* for the others to follow. Suddenly there is a howl of anguish from Brainin. 'No, no, no. That's terrible!' And he goes on to expostulate in German. The problem is that somebody has been taking Verdi's markings at face value again and playing a *fortissimo* just because Verdi asks for one. 'But that sounds awfully crude,' Brainin says, looking pained, and immediately illustrates the way his colleague has just played, followed by the more sensitive way in which he *should* play. Norbert Brainin is like that. He will lay down the law with instant and almost arrogant certainty, pick out anything that any of his colleagues is playing and imitate it on the correct notes, on his own instrument – and, by and large, obtain the acquiescence of the colleague concerned. Sometimes he is wrong and the others tell him so. Sometimes he is right musically but wrong psychologically. On this particular occasion the others acknowledge that he has a point and the offending passage is replayed until the dynamic contrast works more subtly. Forty bars later when Verdi jumps from *pp* to *fff* within two bars, the players are sufficiently accustomed to the idiom that they instinctively increase the intensity of their playing rather than the sheer volume. Nobody writes anything down. Once a point is agreed and rehearsed, it is fixed in everybody's mind.

They are in sight of the end and Brainin is worried about his dentist appointment. But there are still hurdles to cross – in particular the fast and difficult *poco più presto* passage with which the whole piece suddenly spurts to its conclusion (G). Should it be preceded by a slight *ritardando*? Should it begin quickly or gather speed gradually? What about all those sharps and double sharps – are they really in tune? Schidlof and Lovett have a section (H) where their instruments double each other and as they go through it note by note certain inaccuracies reveal themselves.

Time is running out, but Lovett and Schidlof want to sort things out. One of them insists that the other is repeatedly playing flat but the other denies it. Nissel comes up with a solution that is both musically and psychologically helpful. He suggests that he play *his* part with Peter and Martin, for the second violin mirrors the other two parts and the contrary motion that he provides immediately gives the other two a yardstick

(G)

(H)

against which to tune their own playing. The foursome play the whole of the final *presto* once more, positively revel in its final partly syncopated chords (I) – Lovett inventing a new cello variation that Verdi would never have sanctioned – and break up in good spirits. Lovett runs Brainin to his dentist, Nissel goes upstairs to catch up with his office work, and Schidlof, grumbling that he needs to replace his eight-year-old Renault but never has the time to look, waves and drives off to his home in Edgware.

The recording takes place in Munich a week later – by which time Martin Lovett has flown to Israel and back for his father's funeral, and the Quartet has managed to rehearse and perform its all-Brahms concert with Stephen Bishop-Kovacevich at London's Royal Festival Hall.

Recording companies can be a mystery to the outside world and even to many of those closely associated with them. Like cornflakes and soap powder, gramophone records are often merely one of the more immediately tangible products of giant multinational corporations that also interest themselves in much else besides. CBS own not only Columbia Records and the CBS television network but also, among other concerns, Steinway the piano manufacturers – and at one time the New York

Yankees baseball team. Deutsche Grammophon, for whom the Amadeus Quartet have recorded for twenty years or more, is a son of a son of Siemens, the giant German-based concern whose interests extend to almost every imaginable aspect of modern technology. Siemens and the Dutch electronics firm Philips jointly control Polygram which, in turn, is the parent company of a variety of subsidiaries which include the Hamburg-based record company Polydor – one of whose many labels (the principal classical label, in fact) is Deutsche Grammophon. And it is to one of the Munich studios of this company within a group within a conglomerate that the Amadeus Quartet now repairs.

Actually is it not a studio, but the Alter Herkulessaal, one of the old embellished entertainment halls in the collection of palaces and halls known collectively as the Residenz. This home of the former kings and dukes of Bavaria contains several wonderfully ornate halls and rooms, notably the exquisite late eighteenth century Cuvilliéstheater (now completely restored after being largely destroyed in the war by Allied bombing). The Alter Herkulessaal, with its tasteful and largely monochrome drapes and panels and its chandeliers and mirrors, is impressive rather than breathtaking. It is normally used as a rehearsal room for the Munich Philharmonic Orchestra. Part of the ceiling is covered with rolls of curtain material to reduce the echo and much of the floor space taken up with chairs and instruments and music stands. For all the grandeur of the setting, the Amadeus Quartet is placed comfortably into one end of the hall so that its recorded playing will suggest the right combination of intimacy and spaciousness.

The players are in good spirits this particular morning. They have already recorded the Tchaikovsky op. 11 and were faintly surprised at the ease with which this work, which they have never performed in public, was successfully polished off. They easily accomplished their aim of one movement per recording session, and hope that the Verdi, a far harder work which they *have* played in public on and off ever since their début concert in 1948, will prove as straightforward a nut to crack. There is some difficulty getting into the Residenz this morning as Chairman Hua Guofeng of China is in town and is due to have lunch here, in an adjacent wing, in a couple of hours' time. It is a bright, cold October day and, as the members of the Quartet trickle in to the recording company's control room upstairs from the Alter Herkulessaal, having talked their respective ways past the green-coated Bavarian security police, they eagerly help themselves to the coffee and soft drinks of which Deutsche Grammophon seems to furnish a permanent supply. At one end of the control room is a studio console, tape machines, and all manner of other technical necessities. At the other, flanking the coffee and drinks, are two enormous loud-speakers. And in the middle, half a dozen canvas chairs of the sort that film directors sit upon – in this case decorated with the fading signatures of the mighty musicians who have used them. There, more or less legible, are Carlos Kleiber, Teresa Berganza (affectionately known to her appreciative DG colleagues as 'Bonanza'), Martha Argerich, Nathan Milstein, Arturo Benedetti Michelangeli, Peter Schreier and, dating from March 1974, the members of the Amadeus Quartet.

The chat this morning is about Chairman Hua. Tonight he is to attend an opera gala (to which Schidlof and Nissel have been given tickets) and it seems that Richard Strauss's *Salome*, which is short and has no interval, has been substituted for *Madam Butterfly*. Much merriment. Why *Salome*? Perhaps he'll learn something about power and how to cut off the heads of opponents, someone offers, and another adds: 'He probably wanted to watch a strip show!' Maybe the local political boss, Franz-Josef Strauss, who is running for the German Chancellorship next year, wanted to have the name 'Strauss' all over the German press. Somebody mumbles suggestively: 'Should have shown them *Turandot*!'

From somewhere in the direction of Peter Schidlof comes an electronic hum which a good pair of ears would recognize as a perfect 'A'. As a matter of fact it is too perfect being the sound produced by 440 vibrations per second whereas the Amadeus tune their instruments to 442. Schidlof turns a knob very slightly on the electronic device he has picked up from the control desk so as to raise the tone by the scarcely perceptible two vibrations per second. Thoughts and conversation shift slowly from Chairman Hua to music. The production team of Wolfgang Mitlehner and Jobst Eberhardt move towards the console and recording machines respectively, while Frau Kurkovsky, universally known as 'Tchai'kovsky, who has looked after coffee and drinks here for over twenty years, begins to clear away the dirty cups and glasses. Everyone seems to have a nickname. Although the production team and the Quartet use surnames when addressing each other, Nissel kids Mitlehner that he is really Herr Mitleider, the Sufferer. It is time for the Quartet to climb down a marble staircase or two to the distant, invisible, locked hall in which its work is to be done. Twenty minutes into the official session, Mitlehner hears over the loud-speakers in his control room that the four instruments are in tune and the players ready for an opening assault on the first movement of the Verdi Quartet.

It is an E minor *allegro* (A) and the theme is started by the second

(A) Allegro ♩=120

violin to a syncopated and slightly agitated accompaniment by the lower instruments, and is then taken up by the first violin.

As the group gets into its stride, Wolfgang Mitlehner checks his electronic metronome and is amused to notice that they happen to be playing at precisely the prescribed *tempo*. Mitlehner's multi-functional Japanese-made sonal and/or visual metronome (with optional ear-phones) and/or pitch-machine is one of the more intriguing toys in the control room – a natural magnet for Peter Schidlof's attention later in the morning. The movement comes to its end, via some semi-quaver bars for the first violin (B) reminiscent of the storm music in *Rigoletto*.

It's a good take, full of vigour and restless energy, and the Amadeus asks to be let out of its locked cell so that it can come up and listen to what it has just played. At each session the members follow much the same routine. They record a complete movement, come up and listen to it, and then spend the next couple of hours downstairs clearing up this or that passage, leaving it to Mitlehner to decide when and whether there is an acceptable take of each section. In the old days they would come into

(B)

the control room to listen to every bit they recorded and the engineers
would cut the takes together then and there. This was too time consuming
and could have caused the Amadeus to lose something of their flow,
their feel for the overall structure of the piece they were playing. Nowadays, they leave these editorial decisions to Mitlehner; all they do is play
as well as they know how, replay any bits that they themselves are dissatis-
fied with, and accept the judgement of the men in the control room as to
when a section is 'in the can'.

The first movement of the Verdi is difficult and the first take, while
good, has some imperfections that need to be corrected. So down they go
to the sealed *Saal* and start again. From now on it will all be details,
many of them tiny. They start the movement again from the beginning.
No good. Somebody is taking deep and clearly audible gulps of breath
at each of his entries. Perhaps the microphones are too close. Mitlehner
takes the key and leaps off into the abyss. He is back up a few minutes
later having adjusted the mikes and, thereby, the whole acoustic per-
spective. It is now more spacious, slightly more reverberant, and individual

breaths are no longer audible even on the giant speakers in the control room. Off they go once more, Nissel, as ever, setting the perfect *tempo*. Someone has a frog in his throat. Another take. This goes well, though, at the end of it, Brainin thinks that one of the faster chromatic passages was not quite in tune. Mitlehner and Eberhardt find the passage in question and play it back to the Quartet and the errors, if there are any, are scarcely audible. Still, it's worth getting right and the passage is played slowly, note by note, then in *tempo*, and is then recorded. Lovett wants to go back to the reprise of the main subject where the first violin brings back the opening tune accompanied by a series of viola semi-quavers (C).

(C)

Like his colleagues, Lovett is always listening intently to all that goes on, even in passages which do not concern the cello. He thinks that Schidlof is rushing his semi-quavers and getting ahead of Brainin. Or is Brainin holding back the *tempo*? Brainin insists that he isn't. Co-ordination between the two of them is practised and re-recorded. Twenty bars later there is a passage where the violins are playing a *legato* passage against a series of alternated choppy semi-quavers from viola and cello (D).

Lovett thinks that the fiddles should play out more instead of leaving the listener to concentrate on the lower instruments. 'Norbert and Sigi are more important than Peter and me,' he insists, and this section, too, is adjusted after some discussion and experimentation.

The clock shows 12.15. They have been playing now for nearly two hours and are in danger of getting a little stale. Parkinson's law seems to be at work – the studio is booked until 1.00 pm and everybody can think of *something* he would like to do again, and maybe better, since they have time in hand. Upstairs in the control room, attention drifts. Out of the window in the courtyard can be seen an assemblage of magnificent limousines, the grandest of which is sporting the Chinese, German and

(D)

Bavarian flags. Chairman Hua and Minister-President Strauss have just arrived and they and their retinues are moving off to lunch in a part of the Residenz known – ironically, considering how strictly the public gaze is kept at a distance – as the Aquarium. In hot pursuit of the official cars, a number of press buses arrive and debouch great numbers of journalists with legs that only know how to run. Then there are police vans and ambulances that move about in the courtyard for no apparent reason. And, finally, thirty or forty little green Martians whose legs have long since atrophied and given way to little green wheels – these are the Bavarian police outriders who, with nothing much to do until Hua and company reappear after lunch, seem incapable of getting off their motorbikes. It is a strange scene, totally incongruous in the grand setting of an old princely courtyard but, at this stage on this day, it momentarily demands the attention of the recording team more insistently than the discussions and disagreements and checkings and recheckings down in the *Saal* that come up over the speakers in the control room. One or two passages of the Verdi are finally re-recorded (after a delay caused by the noise of the police helicopters outside – clearly audible inside the Alter

Herkulessaal) and then everybody agrees that enough is enough. Eberhardt runs downstairs with the key to let the prisoners out and they look
none the worse for wear. They are satisfied with their morning's work
and look forward to a good lunch.

Let's go Chinese, someone says, in honour of Hua. Lovett is not fond
of Chinese food, so a number of other suggestions are made. Eventually
they settle on a Yugoslav restaurant in Schwabing just beyond the
university. Veronica, a local girl in her twenties whom the Quartet have
known since she was a small child, has joined them in the Residenz and
takes command of the trip to the restaurant. The best way to go is by
underground. Veronica talks about the complicated fare system; it is
almost incomprehensible to the visitor to Munich and barriers to unpaid
travel are nowhere visible, so Veronica also explains, while getting
everybody's ticket, that you can land up with a very heavy fine if you get
caught without having paid!

The station is cool and clean and spacious and the train that soon comes
runs smoothly and quietly. Brainin expatiates on the good sense of the
German people; if only London Transport had put money into moderni-
zing its plant and equipment, the British too might have had a first rate
underground system. In his politics as in his music Brainin has an explosive confidence that can be impressive, endearing even, but also on
occasion irritating. His political instincts are far from liberal. One day
over a meal he tries to persuade Lovett and Nissel that men are inherently
more spiritually developed than women; on another occasion he advances
the case against the admission of homosexuals to the priesthood. On this
particular afternoon, he is decrying the incompetence of British economic
planning – and those within earshot have to admit that he is right. The
efficiency and prosperity of Germany is everywhere in evidence and
visitors from Britain are almost inevitably struck by the contrast this
provides with the shabbiness back home. Brainin's philippics never last
long and most Amadeus meals soon settle down into joke sessions. All
four are accomplished raconteurs and their repertoire of jokes, as of
quartets, is enormous. With Veronica present the risqué stories are
perhaps a more subdued shade of blue than normal, but the tensions
caused by music (and political philosophy) soon give way to hearty
schoolboy guffaws as spicy stories accompany the spicy Serbian dishes
that appear.

As limerick time rolls around, Nissel repeats a splendid rib-tickler by
Peter Warlock (and which is given a *ritardando maestoso* in the last line):

Girls who frequent picture palaces
Have no time for psycho-analysis.
At the mention of Freud
They get very annoyed
And cling to their long-standing fallacies!*

The Quartet disperses after lunch. It is nearly three o'clock and the next recording session is due to begin in a couple of hours' time. One member goes back to the hotel for a brief nap; someone else has a tea date with Munich friends. Lovett is interested in a new three-wave portable radio set that Schidlof has recommended to him and makes for the shopping area of central Munich. At five everyone reassembles in the control room and sips Frau 'Tchai'kovsky's tea and coffee and sour grape and orange juice. Ten or fifteen minutes later, the Quartet are downstairs again in the Alter Herkulessaal preparing to tackle the slow movement of the Verdi quartet.

Things develop much as they did at the morning session: a test 'take' of the whole movement, a communal listen-through in the control room ('Alles ist zu *loud!*' complains Brainin with an air of distaste), and then a couple of hours of re-thinking and re-recording. One take is spoiled by a mysterious but regular clicking sound, someone's ring or button touching a metal chair as he plays a rhythmic *pizzicato* passage; another is interrupted by a member of the Munich Philharmonic Orchestra who needs to collect some things from the *Saal* in preparation for the concert in the larger adjacent hall that they are to give tonight. Once, when the Amadeus were recording the Brahms G minor Quartet op. 25 with Emil Gilels and had just reached the great final piano flurry, the door opened and a night-watchman casually walked his dog right through the recording studio, touching his hat with a pleasant 'good day' as he went, oblivious of what he was interrupting – the players cracked up with laughter and the session went marvellously after that. Nothing quite so dramatic happens on this occasion.

As the players talk and argue and play and replay, Steven Paul, the bouncy, boyish American who is in overall charge of this recording,

---

*The only rival in its capacity to avoid the obvious is Lord Hailsham's favourite:

> *In* A Midsummer Night *playing 'Puck',*
> *A Shakespearean actress got stuck.*
> *But as she'd never heard*
> *Of that four-letter word,*
> *She merely observed, 'What bad luck.'*

breezes into the control room. He has flown in from Paris where he has been wooing Barenboim and Fischer-Dieskau, and has spent much of his day crawling first through the streets of strike-bound Paris (where the traffic lights are all turned off) and then those of a Munich immobilized by the presence of Hua Guofeng. Steven Paul is followed a little later by Frau Kuzaj, neat, greying, attractive, who runs the Munich end of Deutsche Grammophon's activities. Downstairs, the slow movement does not create any insuperable problems and, despite a propensity among the players to 'correct' things that were perfectly acceptable on an earlier take, the session ends well before its appointed time of 8.00 p.m. The players emerge from below and exchange exuberant bear hugs with Steven Paul and Frau Kuzaj. Schidlof and Nissel, all dressed up, rush off to the gala performance of *Salome* while the others think of where to go for dinner.

Brainin, slightly on the outside of the group's sociabilities, wants to attend part of the concert that is about to begin next door – Mozart conducted by Rozhdestvensky. His appetite for music and his capacity to listen with careful discrimination are in a league of their own and when he joins Lovett and the Deutsche Grammophon people at the restaurant (Zur Kanne) an hour or so later he is glowing with the excellence of the performance he has just heard. He is just in time for a magnificent meal with good wine and a lot of funny stories. The party breaks up at around midnight and on the way out of the restaurant everyone admires the old opera programmes and signed photos of singers with which the walls of the restaurant are adorned. Lovett, always his own unabashed self whatever the surroundings, calls over to the others that he has found some cast lists that existed 'courtesy of Dr Goebbels'! Nearly thirty years before, when the Amadeus Quartet first visited Spain, Lovett got the group into hot water by noting that alongside the statutory portrait of Franco was one of an old Spanish general who looked uncannily like Stalin.

Outside it is very cold. Frau Kuzaj takes a taxi to her home just outside the centre of town while Lovett and Brainin, who must be exhausted after an exceptionally long and demanding day, stride purposefully from one end of central Munich to the other and reach their hotel at about 12.30 a.m.

The next day is Saturday. The Quartet meets in the morning and works its way through the third movement of the Verdi. As before, a lot of time is spent on details such as the fast quiet passage that starts at bar 60 (see p. 79, example E), or the phrasing of Lovett's cello solo (see p. 79, example D). When they have finished, the Quartet decides to cancel the evening session and to defer the final movement until the next morning. Nissel and Brainin engage Steven Paul in a vigorous exchange about why Amadeus records are not always as available in music stores as they should be. They also discuss repertoire and what recordings to do over the next couple of years. Meanwhile friends of Schidlof have turned up from Salzburg and everybody eventually adjourns for another splendid meal. The predominant dish is roast goose, the wine is white Franconian. Munich looks magnificent on a clear, cold day such as this – the weather has been spectacularly autumnal throughout the past few days despite reports of storms in much of Europe – and the rest of the day is devoted to walking and talking.

On Sunday, the final movement is recorded fairly painlessly and there is time for the Quartet to listen to some of the takes of tricky passages in earlier movements. Lovett's third movement cello solo comes under scrutiny. Mitlehner and Eberhardt play the opening 'test' take which, while slightly rougher in texture than later, more surgical versions, is also more expressive. Lovett prefers it. So does Steven Paul. Brainin says he thinks it vulgar: worse, it is like a nineteenth century provincial Italian opera singer with no sense of refinement. But it's written operatically, someone offers. Brainin is unrepentant and, after praising the sensitivity of later versions, adds that the first sounds like . . . like . . . like a football fan cheering on the Naples second eleven! Exit Brainin to the bathroom. Lovett and the others smile. They have made their preferences known and are happy to leave to Mitlehner the final judgement about which bits of which takes to use. Mitlehner will, in any case, play back to the Quartet in a few months' time his proposed version of the entire work and they will then be at liberty to propose alternatives to the amalgamation he has made.

For the time being all necessary work has been done; it is time for a final, especially grand, celebratory lunch, courtesy of Polydor. The chosen restaurant is the Königshof, one of Munich's finest. It overlooks one of the gates of the old city, but nearby is a construction site which Nissel seems to recall was already a construction site when he was a boy here fifty years ago. The restaurant is a stone's throw from the scenes of Nissel's childhood and, as he enjoys his meal, his mind wanders back to the park where his parents left him to play in the mornings, and to the brownshirts who made his eight-year-old life a misery as he wended his precarious way to school. Around the table at the Königshof, the conversation veers wildly from the sub-political (an analysis of the reasons for

London's musical pre-eminence, followed by a critique of Arts Council policy) to the super-joky. Nissel quotes Mark Twain's crack that 'when the Mississippi flooded my father floated out on the kitchen door and I accompanied him on the piano'.

By mid-afternoon nobody wants any more to eat or drink and there can scarcely be any more untold jokes. (The members of the Amadeus have a rule that they will always laugh their heartiest when people tell them jokes they already know.) Thoughts turn to home, but the players have plane tickets which force them to stay in Munich one more night. By the following weekend they will be in Lille for the start of a little spin that will take them to Amsterdam, Cologne, Graz and Vienna. They will have a few days at home in between – rehearsing, going to the doctor or dentist, getting the roof fixed and the insurance paid. But for the moment there is nothing to do but pass the time until the next morning. The four have the satisfaction of knowing that two more excellent recordings are 'in the can' and they are in a good, philosophical humour as they say goodbye to their Deutsche Grammophon hosts and friends outside the Königshof. 'See you soon!' everyone cries – and that means Beethoven sessions in January.

It's six weeks later, a bright, clear Monday in mid-December. It looks colder than it is but London is still benefiting from the warm tempteraures that accompanied the previous day's heavy rain. The Amadeus Quartet has only recently got back to London after a busy month on the continent and today it is joined by William Pleeth to give a lunch-time recital in St. John's, Smith Square, in Westminster, a renovated church a stone's throw from the Houses of Parliament from which weekly concerts are broadcast live by the BBC. This particular occasion is a special concert to mark the tenth anniversary of the series. Ten years ago, as now, the Amadeus and Pleeth gave a performance of Schubert's Quintet in C. The work is one they have all played together many times over the years (and in Vienna only the previous week) and no strenuous rehearsing is necessary; 'just a question of re-cleaning the teeth' as Pleeth puts it. An unexpected element of drama is added to the performance by the fact that, a minute or two from the end, a string snaps on Brainin's fiddle, and the audience in the church and around the country has to wait while the BBC's Patricia Hughes demurely explains what has happened and Brainin replaces the broken string with another he has thoughtfully carried in his pocket. Brainin's calm efficiency is all the more remarkable in that he had already broken a string earlier this very morning during the 'teeth-cleaning' rehearsal session.

The Schubert concert ends with the customary plaudits and the members of the Amadeus go their separate ways for a day or two of domesticity. There are clothes to be cleaned, letters answered, friends phoned, family news digested. Schidlof at last finds time to buy himself a new car (and to attend a Queen Elizabeth Hall concert given by the Juilliard Quartet whose viola player, Samuel Rhodes, was at the Schubert concert at St. John's).

By Thursday it is back to work again. The Amadeus has a Queen Elizabeth Hall concert of its own on Sunday and, in keeping with the style of all its London offerings this season, it includes a piano work. They are to perform the piano quintet by César Franck and the pianist is to be one with whom they have perhaps played more than any other, Sir Clifford Curzon. It is at Curzon's magnificent Highgate residence, 'The White House', that the rehearsal is to take place.

Curzon exudes sensitivity and nervous tension. There are great embraces, exuberant risqué jokes, exchanges of familial goodwill. Orders for mid-morning tea and coffee are established. Curzon is in expansive mood. He leads everyone through the house and into his studio where he proudly displays, and lovingly caresses, the cast of Chopin's delicate hand which he now owns and which once belonged to Sacha Guitry. It is kept, alongside a rather inferior cast of Schnabel's hand ('I knew the real thing almost as well as my own,' Curzon muses affectionately as he thinks back to his great teacher), at one end of a large modern studio built as an extension on to Curzon's home. The principal feature of the studio is a vast humpbacked ceiling like the upper third of a tunnel which snugly encapsulates the two grand pianos beneath it while adding richness and reverberation to their tone. At one end of the studio near the hands of Chopin and Schnabel are various other art objects, including an autographed manuscript of the last page of Mozart's G minor Quintet, K 516; at the other, some thirty yards or more away, is an open log fire. In the middle are the two grand pianos, and it is alongside one of these that the Amadeus Quartet will huddle for most of the next three and a half hours.

Energetic conversation continues to flow from Curzon as the members of the Quartet (three of them, actually, as Brainin is late) slowly get down to the business of the day, unpack and tune their instruments, pull Curzon's leg about his latest electronic metronome ('So you've moved into the twentieth century at last!' jokes Schidlof) and, once Brainin has arrived, eventually get seated and ready to play. Curzon has been prepared for at least a quarter of an hour and marvels aloud at the time each of his companions takes titivating. 'You never all sit down together and just set to, do you?' he asks with feigned incredulity. He is not worried because he has known the Amadeus for all of its thirty-odd years and is confident that, once they *are* seated, the miracle will happen. *E Pluribus Unum* – one from many – is the motto of the United States of America. And so it is on this occasion. As soon as bows and hands are poised, a sense of common purpose takes over from the preceding verbal badinage.

Curzon has played the Franck Quintet earlier in the year; the Amadeus have not looked at it since they last joined forces with Curzon for a performance of the work at Aldeburgh in June 1960. By way of refreshing the memory of his friends, Curzon remarks that someone told him the quintet was supposedly a spiritual piece but he thinks it's pretty sensual. Sexy almost. They run through the opening movement with scarcely a break and, for what is essentially a sight-reading exercise for the Quartet, it is not a bad effort. When they reach the end of the opening movement, someone remarks that 'It will all fall into place OK' and nobody demurs.

They go back to the beginning and the real work commences. The quintet opens with a strongly articulated *legato* line (A) from the first violin with pedal accompaniment from the other strings, followed by an expressive 12/8 section for solo piano.

Everyone has something to say to or about everyone else. Brainin would like the string accompaniment to his opening theme to be more pointed. The others are not happy with the bowing he uses. Curzon wants to come straight in with his *espressivo* passage with no 'lift' after the string section and asks if that is acceptable. They play again from the beginning and from the periodic sighs and mutterings of satisfaction it is clear that everyone is pleased with the way the opening section is progressing. Curzon stops and begs his companions to play quieter at one point. Franck has written '*ppp*' and he means it. 'Nadia Boulanger once pointed out to me that this work contains more triple *p*s and triple *f*s than almost anything else in the repertoire,' he says. 'It's a baroque piece, really, and Franck seems to want everything terribly exaggerated.' And sensual, he adds, just in case anyone has forgotten his earlier characterization of the work.

The piece pulses along with great surges of *crescendo* and *diminuendo*. '*Molto espressivo*' writes Franck in one place, '*dolce tenero ma con passione*' in another. Some bits have to be '*dramatico*' and others '*molto tenuto e marcato*'. There is amusement all round at the marking '*senza agitazione*' for it seems

Sir Clifford Curzon at the Amadeus Quartet's 25th anniversary party.

Wilhelm Kempf with the Amadeus.

Recording.

Teaching.

Molto moderato quasi lento

Violine I

Violine II

Viola

Violoncello

Klavier

to suggest, accurately enough, that this is the only passage in the 15-minute first movement that *shouldn't* be agitated! 'I think you should play that bit far more *estinto*,' says Lovett, quoting one of Franck's directions to Schidlof – then jokes that he has no idea what '*estinto*' is supposed to mean.

They are approaching the end of the movement, and the tea and coffee are wheeled in by Sir Clifford's French housekeeper. Conversation during the break is spasmodic, most of the initiatives coming, as throughout the morning, from the irrepressible Curzon. He talks affectionately of Cortot, and suggests that his colleagues try to get a chance to listen to the old 78 r.p.m. recording of the work that Cortot made (adding, 'You'll never want to play it with me again!'). He asks if anyone has seen the new Peter Schaffer play, *Amadeus*, which deals with the supposed poisoning of Mozart by his rival Salieri. Brainin says his wife has seen it; though the history was all wrong and the characters great exaggerations of historical reality, it seems that the play is a real theatrical *tour de force*, particularly Paul Scofield's portrayal of Salieri. 'Oh, that man can do anything with that wonderful voice of his,' says Curzon, and the others agree. Conversation shifts from an avowedly fictional Mozart to a possibly authentic one – the supposed portrait of Mozart, which Curzon has seen, recently picked up in an auction by the Swedish sculptor Torolf Engström.

Curzon's energy is unflagging. As the others settle down for the second movement, he tells them that he has played it recently at two memorial services, one for the actress and writer Yvonne Mitchell and the other for the critic Philip Hope-Wallace. Curzon does not normally like to play a piano in a church, but it does not sound so incongruous if accompanied by a string quartet. 'I won't ask you to play it at my memorial service,' he remarks with a grin, and various death jokes come flying back at him. Brainin has a suggestion for a piano piece that would be perfect for memorial services, and picks out the middle movement from Beethoven's *Pathétique* sonata on his violin. Someone suggests the slow movement from Chopin's *Funeral* sonata – precisely the piece *not* to play, according to Curzon.

They get down to the job in hand and it soon becomes obvious why *this* was the piece chosen for the Mitchell and Hope-Wallace services, for it is slow, spiritual, poignant and graceful. There is also something intimate about it – unlike the Chopin slow march, it would not really do for grand state funerals. It opens with a few bars in which piano chords accompany plaintive descending cries from the first violin (B).

Brainin asks Curzon if he would mind setting a slightly slower *tempo*. Curzon has a request of his own: that Brainin play softer. The *quid pro quo*

(B)

Lento, con molto sentimento

is agreed and they begin again. This time they move on and Curzon, while playing, verbally conducts Brainin and the others. 'Now a little more . . . less on this one . . . that's it, good . . . it's your turn now, Norbert . . . now as beautiful as you can . . . ah, yes, that's perfect.'

'Didn't you like it like that?' asks Curzon, beaming, as they approach the end of the section.

'Yes,' answers Lovett, always prepared to prick any balloon that floats by, 'especially the running commentary in every bar!' Curzon is undaunted, and has a comment or two for Lovett. As the end of the movement approaches, with its sudden reminder of the first movement ('like a burst of sunlight through the clouds,' says Curzon) and its *barcarolle*-like rhythms, everyone is playing well and is happy with the feeling that a hard morning's work is producing good results.

It is nearly 1.30. They can work on the last movement tomorrow afternoon (by which time the Amadeus will have begun rehearsing the two Haydn quartets that are also scheduled for Sunday's concert). That will still leave time on Saturday and Sunday to get things absolutely up to concert level. The morning after the concert, the Amadeus Quartet is off at crack of dawn to Cologne for the last of this year's regular teaching stints there.

Amadeus rehearsals have varied over the years. In the early days the members would put in up to a year's work on a piece before performing it in public and their rehearsal sessions were often far more acrimonious than now. Today, the overwhelming majority of the works they play have been in and out of their repertoire for years and, particularly in the hectic hurry and bustle of a foreign tour, rehearsal often consists of little more than running through the awkward corners of a thoroughly familiar piece and testing a new acoustic an hour or so before the performance. When the Quartet is at home, it tends to rehearse more thoroughly; this is particularly true if it is collaborating with a colleague (like Walter Klien) with whose work it is relatively unfamiliar, or if it is going to play a piece (the Verdi quartet or the Franck Quintet) which it has allowed to become rusty over the years. More is at stake, more can go wrong, and more musical and perhaps psychological problems need to be checked. The most penetrating work, however, is likely to occur when a recording is in the offing, particularly if the piece is a difficult one like the Verdi. Under these circumstances, as we have seen, the experimenting and replaying goes right on up to and inside the recording studio.

Professional musicians at rehearsal are often a disappointment to their admirers. Instead of discussing grand metaphysical questions of interpretation, they usually say little that is not of an immediately practical, down-to-earth nature. The author of a private edition book about one distinguished American quartet tape-recorded rehearsal sessions and reproduced verbatim what was said. The result – the purely *verbal* record – was pretty banal. The principal point about rehearsals is the way the playing improves, not what happens to be said by one player to another. Amadeus rehearsals, however argumentative they might have been thirty years ago, are generally largely wordless now and, while the things said by a Brainin or a Lovett – or a Curzon – might amuse or interest the observer or reader, they represent only a small or relatively insignificant proportion of the musical communication that takes place. In that process of musical communication, the verbally silent can sometimes be musically the most eloquent, and the least argumentative the most persuasive.

TEATRO ALLA SCALA

ENTE AUTONOMO

STAGIONE D'OPERA E BALLETTO 1979
(390ª dalla fondazione del Teatro)

Abbonamento ciclo Schubert
e Fuori abbonamento

MUSICHE DI FRANZ SCHUBERT
II

LUNEDI 19 FEBBRAIO 1979 · ORE 20.30

QUARTETTO AMADEUS

NORBERT BRAININ, violino   **SIEGMUND NISSEL**, violino

PETER SCHIDLOF, viola   **MARTIN LOVETT**, violoncello

PROGRAMMA

FRANZ SCHUBERT   **QUARTETTO IN SI BEM. MAGG. op. 168 D. 112**
Allegro ma non troppo
Andante sostenuto
Menuetto (Allegro)
Presto

QUARTETTSATZ IN DO MIN. op. post. D. 703

QUARTETTO IN LA MIN. op. 29 D. 804
Allegro ma non troppo
Andante
Menuetto (Allegretto)
Allegro moderato

PREZZI (Tasse comprese)
Posto unico numerato di platea o di palco L. **3.000**
Posto numerato di Iª galleria L. **2.000** - Posto numerato di IIª galleria L. **1.000** - Ingresso in piedi L. **500**
Abbonamento per l'intero ciclo di 8 concerti - Posto unico di platea o palco L. **24.000**
Giovani fino a 26 anni sconto 50% su tutti i prezzi

sui biglietti dei posti riservati e acquistati nei giorni precedenti quello dello spettacolo prova d 10% di servizio prenotazione.
A termine di legge è vietato durante lo spettacolo effettuare, anche parzialmente, riprese filmate o registrazioni e scattare fotografie in sala o nei ridotti.
Durante l'esecuzione del concerto è vietato accedere alla platea e alle gallerie. È pure vietato muoversi dal proprio posto prima della fine di ogni pezzo.
In platea non vi sono posti in piedi.
Le gallerie si aprono alle ore 19.30; platea e palchi alle ore 19.45.
Informazioni e prenotazioni alla biglietteria del Teatro: telefoni 807041/2/3/4; orario: dalle 10 alle 13 e dalle 15.30 alle 17.30 (lunedì chiuso).

Nel ridotto palchi e nei ridotto gallerie (ingresso dal Museo Teatrale)
Dal 28 novembre 1978 al 28 febbraio 1979 (orario: 9-12; 14-18) - domenica esclusa)
MOSTRE VIVALDI in collaborazione con ASSESSORATO CULTURA COMUNE VENEZIA
"IL CIMENTO DELL'INVENZIONE - IL SECOLO VIVALDI E IL MELODRAMMA 1650-1750"
"VIVALDI DRESDEN BACH - INFLUENZE ED EFFETTI" - Catalogo ELECTA EDITRICE

Immaginazione e stampa ARTI GRAFICHE CONALDONINI - VIA C. KRAMER, 5 - MILANO

DO WE NOT BLEED?

'It can't last. Those four boys will never stay together once they've each tasted the dizzy heights.' The sort of thing that people were saying – rightly as it proved – about the Beatles in the mid-1960s. And the odds against four highly talented individuals, each with his own powerful personality and considerable artistic gifts, staying together as a continuously successful ensemble over the entire span of a working lifetime must be very long indeed. Personal incompatibility, sickness, the opportunity for one or more members to branch into other fields, or the temptation to sink into routine and therefore oblivion – these are some of the hazards to which almost every small artistic ensemble has succumbed at one time or another. Most marriages have their difficulties and a high proportion end in separation or divorce; but it is rare indeed for a professional marriage between four wholly interdependent artists to have survived as long and successfully as the Amadeus Quartet.

The professional history of the group has been an almost unqualified and uninterrupted success. For over thirty years they have been continuously at the top of their profession, have played in every corner of the globe where good music is appreciated (and many where it was not but is now), and have recorded a sizeable proportion of the standard chamber repertoire. But behind this undoubted success story is a long string of problems that have had to be solved, personal or professional mishaps and misunderstandings that have had to be cleared up, and sheer bad luck that has had to be borne and overcome. The members of the Quartet are human, they catch coughs and colds like the rest of us, have children who get sick and have exam crises and fall in or out of love, and they have all the additional problems of being an internationally celebrated star turn with a demanding public that always expects them to be at their best. Most of us have 'off' days and the members of the Amadeus have their fair share; but while most of us can generally afford to show it, they cannot.

One of the worst crises in the history of the Amadeus Quartet was Siegmund Nissel's serious illness in 1960. During the 1959–60 season he began to feel ill and tired and eventually to get headaches and then double vision. His playing deteriorated as he found it more and more difficult to concentrate either his eyes or his mind on his music. It was a tremendous effort to hold the bow steady when playing long slow notes, or to bounce the bow properly in *spiccato* passages, normally two fairly routine aspects of the violinist's art. He began to be afraid of concerts. Nissel himself thought that it might be nervous tension and that he was heading for a breakdown. After all, the Quartet was by then living a breakneck schedule and only the previous year had gone on a gruelling eight-month world tour. Perhaps the time had come to take stock of the difficult and abnormal life the Quartet was leading and to reduce the group's commitments somewhat.

In a quartet everybody has a personal stake in – and responsibility for – the career and livelihood of three other people. You sink or swim together. How do you react when one member is palpably not pulling his weight? Human sympathy, of course, if he is definably ill. But suppose it crosses your mind that maybe he just can't stand the pace? Do you tell him? Scold him? Cajole? Cut down on the number of commitments? Consider the possibility of replacing him? Or even of disbanding the ensemble? At the outset little of this was voiced, but the others would have been less than human if this welter of painful thoughts had not flickered across their collective consciousness. Something had to be said. But what? Normally, it is vital in a quartet that everyone should feel free to criticize the playing of everyone else; only by mutual criticism and the capacity to accept it can the highest standards be maintained. But such criticism must never be destructive. It is obviously counter-productive to criticize a colleague for failing to do things that he simply lacks the equipment to do. Were Nissel's current failings in this category? None of the others knew for sure. Nissel himself continued to assume that his problems were of a temporary nature and that he would pull himself together over the summer weeks while the others were on holiday and all would then be well. And if all wasn't well? That was a mental bridge that nobody was prepared to cross.

Nissel is a man of iron resolve. Astonishingly, he played through the season and, by sheer grit and determination and the most acute sense of duty towards his colleagues, ensured not only that the Quartet did not have to cancel a single concert but also that their playing continued to be to their usual high standard. Press reviews from that excruciatingly difficult time give no indication of the agony that the Quartet as a whole and Nissel in particular was suffering. But as soon as the last concert was played, Nissel went to his doctor again. Doctor and patient had both assumed until then that the problems were primarily psychiatric but by now the doctor began to suspect that the causes might be physical. At any rate, there would be no harm in trying to find out. 'Forget the mind,' he said to his startled patient, 'let's look at the head.'

Norbert Brainin was on holiday in Italy when the news reached him that Nissel was found to have a brain tumour and was so aghast at the news that he ran to the bathroom and was sick. Nobody knew yet whether the tumour was benign or malignant nor, if the former, what its long-term effects might be. In the event, it was benign and was successfully removed and the rest of the Quartet returned from their holidays happy in the knowledge that their friend and colleague was fully on the mend. They fulfilled all their concert engagements, sometimes playing trios and sometimes piano quartets with Denis Matthews and others. By late autumn, Nissel was able to rejoin them and life went on for the Amadeus almost as if nothing had happened. But the incident was a reminder to Nissel in particular and to the Quartet in general of the frailty of human life and institutions and of the extraordinary good luck which, in conjunction with high talent, good organization, good will, and a vast amount of endless hard work, had helped the Amadeus Quartet to reach the heights and stay there so long.

There have been other problems from time to time, some more serious than others. One absurd incident which threatened to bring the life of the Quartet to a precipitate end occurred in 1975 when Norbert Brainin sat on a finger. He was in his car one day, put his left hand underneath him to straighten the back of his coat, and accidentally buckled the middle finger under the whole of his not inconsiderable weight. At the time he did not pay much attention to the incident and presumed that the slight feeling of strain in the finger would disappear within a day or two. But it did not. Indeed, he found that his normally agile violin fingering became more and more laboured as the pain in the finger got worse. In the event, it transpired that he had what was called a 'mallet' finger; he had torn the ligaments that cover the knuckle just below the finger-tip and link the muscles in the lower and upper parts of the finger. In order for these to grow back together again he would have to keep the finger absolutely straight for many weeks, so for two months, he had to wear – day and night – a little metal splint over his finger to keep it rigid. There was absolutely no question of playing the fiddle; eating and washing and dressing were quite hard enough. At first, the ligaments did not look as though they were going to knit together again and, as at the time of Nissel's illness fifteen years before, serious concern was felt – if not expressed – that the days of the Amadeus Quartet might now be numbered. However, the Crisis of Norbert's Finger, like various other crises great and small that had preceded it, was weathered successfully. The incident and recuperation took place over the spring and early summer period so that relatively few concert cancellations were necessary. When the 1975–6 season began, Brainin was able to play again just as before.

The Quartet has a very good record of fulfilling its commitments. In over thirty years out of a total of over 4,000 concerts it has cancelled perhaps fifty or sixty. There is nothing shameful in cancelling an engagement if *force majeure* intervenes, and the Amadeus naturally takes out non-appearance insurance. But the players hate cancelling – even on occasions when they probably should. The most notorious such occasion, one which still occupies a bitter seat in the memory, is their New York début in 1953.

Once the Amadeus Quartet had been successfully launched in 1948 and had started to tour abroad a couple of years later, it was only a matter of time before it would go to the United States. This was where the big audiences and the big money were to be found; if any artists were to 'make it', they had to do so in the USA and, in particular, in New York City. The auguries seemed good. The Amadeus had already made several discs with the American Westminster company and the Quartet's New York producer, the Englishman Jimmy Grayson, wanted it to help promote the records with a concert tour.

They set off in good spirits delighted at the number of American engagements that awaited them and understandably confident that their first tour of the USA would, like everything else they had done so far, be a triumph. The highlight of their tour, the one concert above all others that they *had* to get right, the one that would get all the reviews that really counted, was their New York début. This was due to be given, early in their tour, at New York's Town Hall. Later on they were to return for another New York concert, at Columbia University. For their New York début, however, they would pull out all the stops. But New

York beat them to it and pulled out a few of its own. For one thing the Town Hall concert was cancelled (for reasons that had nothing to do with the Amadeus). This meant that the group's New York début would now have to be the later appearance at Columbia.

On the night before the Columbia concert, the foursome embarked for New York by train from Cincinnati. The following afternoon, as the train eventually approached New York, Brainin was fumbling about in his case when he cut the ring finger of his left hand across the top of the nail on a razor. He was in a panic and, as soon as the boys arrived in New York and checked into their hotel, Brainin rushed off to a doctor who gave him a bandage. In the late afternoon, the players took a taxi from their hotel to Columbia, were welcomed by the management, and went straight into the hall, intending to do a little pre-concert warm-up – only to discover to their total consternation that they had left the case containing all their music in the taxi! Schidlof had a cousin in New York who might be able to provide them with copies of the music they were to play that evening and, after a delay that seemed interminable, this was duly delivered and the concert proceeded as scheduled. But it did not go well. The foursome knew the Mozart scores inside out, of course, but felt ill at ease playing from unfamiliar, unmarked copies where the page turns came at all the wrong places. Things were not made any easier by the fact that the music stands provided by the Columbia management were uncomfortably high. The worst thing, however, was that when Brainin took off his bandage he found that the broken skin and nail of his injured finger would not stand up to the pressure of playing so that by the interval his violin was dripping with blood.

There were compensations, the most touching of which was that the taxi driver discovered the music in his cab and brought it to Columbia where it was reunited with its owners just in time for the final work. Furthermore, there was a good and appreciative audience largely composed of people who, in contrast to some of the provincial audiences to whom the Amadeus had recently performed, obviously knew and loved serious music. But the occasion was demoralizing. It says a lot for the courage and professionalism of the Quartet that they played the concert as well as they evidently did, for their notices were mixed rather than adverse. But the whole experience was a nightmare with repercussions that threatened to cast a dark shadow far into the future. 'You see,' their American agent was able to say in future years, pointing with a sigh to the less favourable Columbia reviews, 'you see, I simply can't offer you more than X dollars for Y concerts during your next tour.'

As it happened, some of the harm done by the Columbia début was erased at the outset of their very next visit to the States a year later. In March 1954, Virgil Thompson, one of America's most respected composers and a formidable critic, reviewed an Amadeus concert in the New York *Herald Tribune*: 'The Amadeus Quartet, playing yesterday in Town Hall, made some of the loveliest string music that this devotee has ever heard ... They played quartets of the great Viennese tradition with so natural a grace and such a sweet warmth that one had the feeling constantly "This is how those pieces really go".' He went on to praise their 'utterly convincing *tempos*' and 'subtle lilt of rhythm', their 'beauty of sound' and 'clean execution' and concluded with the remark that the Haydn C major, op. 54 No. 2 and Schubert's *Death and the Maiden* quartets 'have rarely in my experience sounded more natural or felt more true'. Virgil Thompson's review was reproduced in all their publicity material, and was even referred to by admiring critics who praised later Amadeus appearances. When the foursome ended their second American tour and boarded the *Queen Elizabeth* for the voyage home seven weeks later, they had the comfort of knowing that the damage done by their chapter of accidents the previous year had been somewhat offset by their glowing reception in America this time around. But their concert at Columbia University in 1953 undoubtedly did them a lot of harm and its shadows continued to pursue them for many years. Should they have cancelled the concert? Maybe. But then, it *was* their New York début.

For an ensemble that depends for its viability on four different people being on tip-top form all the time, it is astonishing that the Amadeus has not cancelled more engagements than it has. There are a lot of things that can go wrong and sooner or later many do. Most people, chamber musicians included, get their fair share of whatever infections are going the rounds, and only one member of a quartet has to have a bout of gastric flu or an attack of hayfever (such as once forced Martin Lovett to bow out of the latter half of their first tour of Germany) for the group to be put out of action or for radical last-minute re-programming to be concocted. The Amadeus Quartet, unlike an operatic or orchestral promoter, cannot bring in last minute substitutes. At the time of Nissel's illness, they experimented for a while in the semi-privacy of a summer festival at the Schloss Elmau in southern Bavaria with Suzanne Rozsa as second violin. But for all her brilliance as a violinist it soon became clear that the sense of ensemble the group had achieved with Nissel after twelve years together could not quickly be reproduced with another player.

When one considers the constant variations of physical condition to which the members of the Amadeus Quartet subject themselves as they fulfil their endless round of commitments, year in and year out, working in overheated hotel rooms or concert halls here, dashing to catch a plane that will take them to a totally different climate there – the sheer physical adaptability and resilience of the four men is something to be wondered at. It has often been remarked that one of the characteristics shared by almost all people at the top of a public profession is a degree of mental and physical stamina that most others are not able to match. What have people like Georg Solti, Zubin Mehta and Placido Domingo got in common with Winston Churchill, Henry Kissinger and Björn Borg? Answer: a passionate commitment to the job they have undertaken and a supreme confidence in their own ability to fulfil its heavy demands – plus superb good health, and the ability to work hard on little sleep and to sleep deeply when the opportunity presents itself. All these qualities the members of the Amadeus Quartet have in abundance.

In addition to the abnormal physical demands imposed by their busy life, the musicians of the Quartet are also vulnerable to all the vicissitudes of modern travel. As anyone who frequents the world's airports will know to his chagrin, flights are frequently delayed so that travel between the various cities of Europe, for instance, can often necessitate far more time spent on the ground than in the air. The members of the Quartet have hair-raising stories of delayed flights and mislaid baggage, and of concert commitments they only just managed to fulfil, with no time for rehearsal, changing into their evening dress at the airport toilet or in the taxi. But very few (a notable exception being the occasion on which the Empire State Express was derailed outside Utica, N.Y.) of dates they actually failed to meet.

Assuming that all four players are safely delivered in good time, health and spirits to the hall, there are still all sorts of unpleasant surprises that the fates can have in store. Brainin recalls an occasion when, in the middle of a public performance of a Beethoven quartet, he turned his music and noticed, aghast, that the next page was missing Nobody likes to have his memory put to the test under such conditions but he passed this particular ordeal successfully. The Amadeus, like most quartets, plays from printed parts. A copy of the full score is often around when the players rehearse, but the print is usually too small and the page-turns too frequent for use in performance. If they memorized everything they played their concert repertoire would shrink to a fraction of its normal size (though the trauma of the lost music at the time of their New York début would not have occurred). Thus, it seems reasonable on balance to play from parts and each member is responsible for keeping his own and bringing along whatever is needed. It is not often that somebody loses or forgets his music, but it has happened. At a charity concert at the Wigmore Hall in 1964 they were about to play Mozart's *Hunt* quartet, only to discover that one part was missing. HUNT THE QUARTET was the headline in the *Daily Mail* the next morning.

There are other things that can threaten to bring even the most confidently and carefully planned and executed occasion to an abrupt halt. The Amadeus were once playing the Beethoven op. 127 in Staines Town Hall, in Middlesex, when the platform lights suddenly lost almost all their voltage. The foursome managed to play through to the end without raising an eyebrow between them. 'We could have played it in complete darkness,' Brainin told the press afterwards when asked if the sudden blackout had put them off – though there was doubtless a touch of bravado (whistling in the dark?) in his comments. Then there is the possibility of a broken string. Every player knows the fear that a string will snap in mid-performance and, on the rare occasions that it does, the awkwardness of the event – to say nothing of the awesome silence that emanates from the expectant audience – can seriously affect the concentration of the ensemble.

When Brainin's string snapped during the 1979 broadcast of Schubert's C major Quintet from St. John's, Smith Square, there was an obvious place in the score from which to recommence once the string had been replaced (and the BBC were able to knit the original and second versions together in time for the rebroadcast a few days later). But the members of one distinguished American ensemble still shudder at the memory of a string that snapped thirteen minutes into a performance of an exceptionally complex fifteen-minute modern work. There was no 'break' point at which to recommence and, after a lively and even acrimonious debate in full view of the audience, they decided to go all the way back to the beginning and, their concentration broken, proceeded to give a greatly inferior performance of the entire work.

The Amadeus Quartet were in Hong Kong when, on two successive evenings, the performance was interrupted by a broken string. The first night it was Brainin, the second Schidlof. The tension in the hall on the second occasion was such that players and public alike wondered, during the forced interruption, whether the concert could possibly continue with any semblance of musical concentration on or off the platform. Fortunately, Lovett had the presence of mind to announce to the assembled multitude that they might be interested to know that, over the years, the record showed that there *had* been Amadeus concerts at which nobody broke a string all evening! There was much laughter – from relief as much as amusement – and the rest of the evening was an artistic and emotional catharsis greatly enjoyed by all concerned.

Audiences can, of course, cause their own disruptions. Each member of the Amadeus Quartet has a story or two to tell about an eccentric member of the audience. One player recalls the brief appearance of a disconcertingly low *décolletée* gown strategically placed directly below his music stand at the beginning of an Amadeus performance in Brussels. After sweating his way through the first piece, and just as he was beginning to wonder how he would be able to concentrate on his music, the gown, its occupant and her companion swaggered out as they realized that they were at the wrong concert and their tickets were for the pop group next door. Lovett remembers one bizarre occasion when someone suddenly got up during a concert in Columbus, Ohio, walked deliberately down to the platform, and stood by the cello staring at him from a distance of about nine inches.

The worst audience offences, the ones for which the Amadeus feel little amusement or compassion, are the bouts of coughing that erupt every now and then. Anybody can suffer from an attack of uncontrolled coughing but nobody has to stay hacking away in a concert audience and ruin the performance for everybody else. At one period, Brainin went through a phase of asking – telling – noisy audiences to stop coughing, and on occasion even stopped in mid-performance to issue his angry order. It worked like magic, of course, but it is debatable whether the silence that followed was a genuine reflection of the audience's renewed and uninterrupted attention to the music. Andrew Porter, writing in the *New Yorker* on 14 May 1979, quoted the instruction from programme books in London's Royal Festival Hall: 'During a recent test in the Hall, a note played *mezzoforte* on the horn measured approximately 65 decibels (dB (A)) of sound. A single "uncovered" cough gave the same reading. A handkerchief placed over the mouth when coughing assists in obtaining a *pianissimo*.

'There are times when one wishes New York concerts began with a little lecture-demonstration, kin to those given by air hostesses before take-off: an exhortation to refrain from obtrusive bodily movement; an instruction on how to stifle coughing and on techniques for delaying it during passages when the music is very quiet; perhaps an observation that after certain pieces a brief moment of silence can show truer appreciation of a work and its interpreters than a "Bravo!" bawled while the last notes are still dying away. It might be a good idea to have a special foot-tappers' section (heavily carpeted) on the lines of the smoking section in an airplane.' With all of which the members of the Amadeus Quartet would undoubtedly agree.

Occasionally, the Amadeus Quartet encounter problems on a scale far beyond their own particular careers and lives, and far beyond anything that could have been planned or even anticipated. Global crises and catastrophes blow up and force themselves upon the attention of every-body, even travelling musicians. For the most part, the members of the Quartet go about their business largely independent of the great world of politics. They are not unaffected by politics, of course, and are fully aware of such matters as alterations in tax laws or exchange rates, issues that might have a bearing on their contracts and incomes. Their own political inclinations tend to be somewhere on the moderate liberal left, though Brainin can give vent to some pretty dyed-in-the-wool utterances if sufficiently provoked, while Nissel's sophisticated political intelligence makes any simple label like 'socialist' grossly inadequate. Generally speaking, however, their preoccupations are not political and, except when a person like Edward Heath gives them special attention, the world of politics reciprocates by leaving them alone.

Occasionally, however, it does not. During their world tour of 1958, for instance, they had originally intended to include Indonesia on their itinerary, but reports of regional discontent and the proclamation and eventual military crushing of an anti-Sukarno government in West Sumatra and North Celebes forced them to change their plans and visit South Africa earlier than intended.

Even more dramatic was the assassination of President Kennedy on 22 November 1963. The Amadeus Quartet were on tour in the United States at the time and were at St. Louis *en route* to Louisville when the appalling news came through from Dallas. There could be no question of simply going ahead with that evening's scheduled concert in Louisville as though nothing had happened; the intense emotions of the moment called for a special response. After much hurried consultation and some frantic telephone calls, they decided to substitute for the Louisville pro-gramme Haydn's *Seven Last Words*, an hour-long work of seven move-ments each built around a quotation read by a narrator (in this instance a local Catholic priest) from Christ's *Father Forgive Them*. The occasion was deeply moving for all concerned and the Quartet repeated the concert at its next engagement too and, in the event, gave a pair of concerts that everybody felt were absolutely appropriate under the exceptional circumstances.

In a long and busy professional life, the range and number of things that can go wrong are impossible to enumerate, and the Amadeus Quartet has again and again proved its toughness as well as its flexibility when faced with the unexpected. But the most serious affliction that could descend upon – and spell ruin for – an ensemble like the Amadeus Quartet is one from which they have mercifully been relatively immune but which has broken up countless similar bodies: personal incompatibility.

The members of the Amadeus Quartet, like the partners in a good marriage, are far from being carbon copies of each other. On the contrary, they have sharply contrasting personalities which interlock in ways that enable the whole to be not only musically but also temperamentally more than the sum of its parts. This is the key to the question that everybody asks about them: how is it that, against all the odds and all the precedents, they have stayed together for so long and with such success? That they are all fine, dedicated musicians of the highest calibre goes without saying. Less obvious but of almost equal importance is the complementarity of temperaments and personal qualities with which they are blessed. The balance for which every marriage partner aims – to participate in a genuinely joint enterprise while at the same time retaining one's individuality – has been achieved with a rare degree of equilibrium by the members of the Amadeus Quartet.

It was not something that they worked at or analysed or were even terribly conscious of in the early days. All they knew then was that they had a musical job to get on with and that the more success they had as an ensemble the greater the personal and professional stake each had in continuing to (so to speak) play his part. There were problems, rows even. 'Bedlam wasn't in it,' says one friend from the early days who recalls listening 'in fascinated horror at the shouts, bangs and yells' that would emanate from Imogen Holst's studio at Dartington when the Amadeus was in there rehearsing in the late 1940s and early 1950s. Entire rehearsal sessions would occasionally be lost as argument would rage over a matter of *tempo*. Much of this was a product of genuine musical disagreement, but some of it was sparring for position, attempts to assert individual leadership and authority.

Even when the tensions were at their worst, however, there was never any question of splitting up. The battles were often fierce and ungloved and the energy might pour out at any time from any of the four corners. Everything was open to question. But the foursome knew at the time and are still convinced that by risking all they also stood to gain all. Every argument concluded represented a further cementing of what was from the outset a fundamentally compatible relationship. 'Every time we had a fight,' they acknowledge nowadays, 'we were, in effect, trying to work our way through a potentially divisive aspect of our musical or personal relationships towards greater harmony.' Tempered by fire, the bond thus created was undoubtedly all the stronger.

Within a few years, all four members of the Quartet had become sufficiently confident of their own musicianship and of their own indispensable place in the ensemble not to need to flaunt personal independence for its own sake. Occasional flare-ups continued, of course; but they were usually about the sort of things that were worth flaring up about, and always came to be doused by the instant application of good sense.

The tensions the members of the Amadeus have had to learn to live with result not only from their individual temperaments and the determination to make the highest standard of music together, but also from the collective life-style their very success has imposed upon them. Most people sometimes have to subordinate their occasional resentments and frustrations to the broader interests of the private, professional or public relationships into which they have entered. Furthermore, there is nothing unusual in a person pursuing an unbroken career in a single field for the entire span of a working life. But in what other profession does a person normally have only three regular workmates? Three workmates, moreover, whose identity does not vary in over thirty years and with whom one spends over 300 days out of every 365! The only remotely comparable situations – other than that of the three sleepless, eyelidless prisoners in Sartre's *Huis Clos*, an allegory about Hell – are those of master and servant or husband and wife.

Do the members of the Amadeus ever feel locked into something that, for all its obvious attractiveness, nevertheless restricts their individual opportunities? Norbert Brainin, for instance, began a career as a soloist and still occasionally directs and plays concertos with groups like the Cambridge Players and the Scottish Baroque Ensemble. Peter Schidlof, similarly, has become one of the most sought-after interpreters of Berlioz' *Harold In Italy* as well as more modern works such as the Bartok and Walton concertos. And the two of them together are among the most distinguished performers of Mozart's *Sinfonia Concertante* which they give some half dozen times each year. Don't these occasional outside musical activities set in motion the subversive thought, as the individuals concerned face the Quartet's gruelling schedule, 'Oh, God, not *Razumovsky Three* or *Death and the Maiden* again! And no chance to do the *Kreutzer* or *Spring* Sonata or perform this or that concerto with Giulini or Solti or Karajan . . .'?

The answer from all four is a resounding 'No!' The Quartet always comes first and is never felt to be a restriction. Their constant appetite for quartet work is, of course, refreshed by the sheer size of their repertoire which ensures that the old favourites do not, in practice, recur that often in a season. Furthermore, they spend the whole of their professional lives in constant communion with what they all consider 'the world's greatest music'. This is no public relations rationale; as eminent a judge of musical matters as Sir William Glock agrees that 'however great a few of Mozart's symphonies are and many of Haydn's and most of Beethoven's, none of them quite compares with their greatest chamber works'. If Lovett or Schidlof, or even the two violinists, had concentrated on solo careers, they would have found themselves playing a standard repertoire of a score of major works instead of seventy or eighty. Finally, in the words of Emanuel Hurwitz, who has been the distinguished leader of orchestras large and small and is now leader of the Aeolian Quartet, 'Playing in a string quartet is the most exacting thing of all, a medium that has no mercy – and yet it is also the one that offers the most gratifying musical rewards to anyone who has talent and perseveres.'

But the insatiable appetite for work displayed by the members of the Quartet no doubt has psychological as well as aesthetic explanations in that the Quartet provides a degree of routine, and also of communality which in the business professions, for instance, nobody would find any reason to question and which the members of the Amadeus clearly cherish. For the three who had lived such intolerably disrupted lives during the decade before their ensemble was formed, the very stability of quartet life has always ranked high as an important psychological attraction. In addition, there is probably a sense of communal fulfilment in the performance of chamber work that might be lacking in the lonely and exposed world of the soloist; psychologically, as well as musically, ensemble playing feels just right to the members of the Amadeus.

If the four have long since learned to benefit from the communal exercise in which they are engaged and have largely ironed out the major disagreements between them, they have managed to avoid the opposite extreme and have not lost their individual personalities. Far from it! It may be true (as Lovett says) that if two Amadeus members were independently and separately coaching a young ensemble – even in music the Amadeus had not itself played – they would each make largely the same points. But it is also true that each member continues to contribute to it his own musical ideas and his own personal gifts and insights. And just as the similarities of musical outlook between the four have been turned to their communal advantage, so their differences of personal outlook have proved beneficial. What once could seem potentially so destructive has now become an asset.

In the early years, everybody did a bit of everything. The Amadeus Quartet was not only a musical ensemble of the highest professional calibre but it also soon became a complicated and sensitive machine requiring the most detailed and careful attention if its principal activity, that of making music, was not to suffer. By the early 1950s much of the regular scheduling and the negotiation of fees was undertaken by the group's agent, Ibbs and Tillett, but Ibbs would check every detail with the group. In those days Nissel, the one natural manager among them, took all this arduous liaison work upon his own shoulders. Nissel liked everything to be a 'Quartet decision' which meant that valuable time was often devoted to the logistical problem of getting everyone to consider, agree, and pronounce upon the latest proposal. Should they go to Germany again so soon after the previous visit? Should they refuse to do the *Dissonance* quartet three times in two weeks? Did they have to accept pianist X in city Y? Could they accept a smaller fee or try for a higher one for this or that engagement? Should more be spent on advertising the following year? How would some new engagement affect the way their travel arrangements were shaping up?

These and similar questions ate so deeply into time that should have been devoted to music-making and imposed such a strain on Nissel that the Quartet decided to make their decisions more rationally if less democratically. Brainin would take on all the principal questions of where and what to play, Schidlof the travel arrangements, Lovett everything to do with publicity, while Nissel would still retain all the arduous and time-consuming business and accountancy matters. It was a very rough and ready division of labour with vast areas of overlap, and in all four areas many important decisions could still only be made in consultation with the others. But it lifted what was threatening to become an intolerable load from the shoulders of the Quartet as a whole, and Nissel in particular, and shared the burdens around somewhat.

Nissel's contribution to the human dynamics of the foursome has always been his patient capacity to understand and consider various points of view and then to steer the most sensible course. He once said in a BBC radio feature that one of the most important qualities a second violinist in a quartet must have is reliability – to which Hans Keller adds, with Nissel's musicianship specifically in mind, the supreme gift of empathy, the ability to listen to the individual voices around him and constantly to adjust his own playing so as to help the ensemble as a whole to maintain its overall balance and shared intention. Fellow musicians say that if you go to an Amadeus concert and shut your eyes it is often impossible to distinguish Nissel's playing from Brainin's – a fact that speaks volumes not only for Nissel's glorious playing but also for his immensely subtle musicianship. Empathy – musical and personal – he has in abundance. The tensions and arguments that have erupted from time to time between the members of the Amadeus Quartet have again and again been defused by Nissel and from the outset it was he who took on the lion's share of the Quartet's management. In later years, once the division of labour had been worked out and Nissel confined himself largely to accountancy and business questions, he conducted these with exemplary thoroughness and integrity. Nissel has a greater perception of what the Quartet should or should not undertake than any of his colleagues, and this has often placed him in the awkward position of being the man who has to persuade the others to say 'no'. 'If after one of our concerts I really wanted to know how things had gone, I'd go to Sigi for the most objective judgement,' says Lovett. The only time Nissel is reputed to have lost his cool in public was when, at a party in New York, he and a friend were roundly turned on by some aggressive dowager for daring to defend second violinists. As Sigi tells it, he became very flustered – until it transpired that the lady had misheard the conversation she had so rudely interrupted and had thought the two men were justifying 'sex'n'violence'.

So successful have the members of the Amadeus Quartet been in integrating their personal and professional gifts that it is a matter of some wonder that each of the four also has a family life of his own. Life for the Amadeus wives has not always been easy, and some of the Amadeus children have shown occasional signs of straining at the paternal bit ('why should I do what daddy says when he's never even here?'). Each member of each family has had an unusual personal adjustment to make.

If you are married to a man with a busy, jet-setting career, you might opt for the traditional role of housewife, mother and help-meet – in which case you will, like Katinka Brainin (from Breslau) or Margit Schidlof (from Sweden) have to run the risk that your life will contain days and weeks of domestic loneliness, particularly once your daughter (for they each have one) has grown up. Alternatively, if you are the energetic and ambitious type, you might try to combine wifehood and motherhood with a career of your own as a violinist and music teacher (like Suzanne Rozsa Lovett) or social statistician and magistrate (like Muriel Nissel, the only English-born Amadeus wife) – though the conflicting demands of your full-time professions, your daughter and son (which each has), and your absent-then-present-then-absent-again husband must from time to time impose strains, both physical and emotional.

All four families have always accepted the overriding importance of the Quartet, of course; that is, after all, where most of their bread and butter has come from. But the men have occasionally felt irritated by the length and frequency of their trips away from home, while the wives and children have not all come through the decades totally unmarked. On balance, nevertheless, marriage and parenthood have obviously worked well in all four households though, as with the Quartet itself, the successful interweaving of personal give and take has in each family turned out better in practice than anyone might on the face of it have had a right to expect. As everybody gets older and possibly wiser, domestic problems that were once agonizing are now more easily solved or bypassed. Everybody knows that the sacrifices have been in a good cause, one from which everybody has stood to benefit immeasurably.

As the Amadeus Quartet marches confidently on through its fourth decade together, as three of its members approach their sixtieth birthdays, and as the Amadeus children leave home and the grandchildren begin to appear, some thought is inevitably directed towards the future. How long can the Amadeus last, given the frantic pace and impeccable standards it has set itself? Five more years? Ten? Will it end with a bang or a whimper? The sudden death or disability or retirement of one member, or a gradual communal inclination to play less and relax more? When Cecil Aronowitz, with whom the Amadeus had played the Mozart quintets for thirty years, died in 1978, the foursome were reminded by a cruel and unexpected blow that time is not standing still, and they would obviously be foolishly short-sighted if they did not give some thought to ways of winding down their activities in the years ahead.

They plan, or at least say they intend, to stay at home a little more and to give fewer concerts. This is something they have been promising themselves for many years, but the combined blandishments of agents, concert societies and broadcasting and recording organizations have in the past broken down the foursome's resolve. At one time they gave as many as 150 performances a year. From 1966 it was generally just above the 100 mark while from 1980 the aim is about 75 a season.

They still visit a dozen or fifteen countries every season.

If they manage to get the number of concert engagements down, they will probably increase the amount of teaching they do. All four are accomplished teachers and clearly get and give a lot of pleasure passing on to young players the fruits of their own experience. They do not do much teaching of individual instrumentalists but have all coached a great many younger quartets.

Students describe Lovett as immensely enthusiastic, bursting with in-fectious good cheer, and as thrilled as those on the receiving end at any improvement he feels he has helped to bring about. Something of the eternal student himself, Lovett still loves to practise unaccompanied Bach – his favourite composer and the one whom, as a quartet player, he misses most. Lovett's patient receptivity to the problems faced by less accomplished and less experienced players gives his teaching a refreshing warmth and vitality.

Schidlof ('Eagle Ears' one awestruck young player calls him) is perhaps the toughest of the four in the sense that he is less prepared than any of his three colleagues to ignore errors on matters of technical detail, though his feel for the overall flow of a piece is never subordinated to these niceties. Schidlof's mind is possibly the most technical of the four Amadeus players. On a BBC radio programme in 1978 he said that the one book he would like to have on his desert island would be an instru-ment-making manual. He is also a perfectionist. 'If I were a record producer,' he says, 'I'd never pass anything!' Schidlof's unique blend of technical perfectionism allied to musical flair of the highest order can lead a quite moderate student ensemble to approach standards of which it might never have considered itself capable.

Players who have been coached by Nissel agree that his teaching shows a great refinement and subtlety of musical intelligence at work; of the four he is perhaps the one most concerned with delicacies of balance and shading. Never one to give undue emphasis to this or that individual line or instrument or to push students into playing something the particular way he or the Amadeus Quartet play it, Nissel imparts to those he coaches (in the words of a grateful beneficiary, Levon Chilingirian) 'a broad and immensely well-informed awareness of every aspect of the score as a whole, its mood and its character'.

And Brainin? 'A benevolent Buddha' is how one appreciative student describes him. Brainin who can be so tough – almost a bully – with his professional colleagues, is helpfulness itself with younger and less experienced players – full of energy, full of imagination, and overflowing with encouragement. All four members of the Amadeus Quartet impress the students they have taught, and all show a depth of musical understanding and a capacity to see the problems of their own particular instrument as part of a broader endeavour which younger players have described as a revelation.

Teaching used to be an infrequent and irregular activity but has now become institutionalized in the form of a regular monthly visit to Cologne where, largely at the instigation of Max Rostal, they have become professorial colleagues of their own former mentor. Although they are worked very hard at the Hochschule für Musik and are often coaching a quartet each for a scarcely interrupted ten-hour stint, the Cologne arrangement does also mean that they can each develop some regularity and even continuity of social contacts, open a local bank account and, in general, regard Cologne as closer to a home than a one-night stand.

Even now, the Amadeus Quartet is not without ambition. There are new places the members would like to play, notably China. And works. They all regret that they have only performed three of Bartok's six quartets (the last three) and hope that they might have a chance of tackling the others. They also mention Debussy, Ravel and Janacek. Schidlof, whose solo work has led him to make a number of memorable forays into the field of contemporary music, wonders aloud whether the Quartet should not at long last try to get fully to grips with Schoenberg, Berg and Webern. And there are still works from the standard repertoire (such as Haydn's six quartets op. 33) which they would like to record.

At the time of writing, each of the four has an undiminished appetite for work. But each also talks wistfully about things he would like to have done if he had had the time – things that might still be possible in the future. All four feel that they have been so busy playing music that they have not spent enough time listening to it. Sigi and Muriel Nissel go to the opera whenever they can while Schidlof loves to listen to the songs of Schubert. An interviewer once asked the Amadeus if they ever saw other quartets. 'Yes, in airport lounges,' was Lovett's characteristic and only slightly exaggerated reply.

Lovett is a regular cinema-goer and enjoys reading the great works of literature. He once contemplated undertaking some sort of university-level Shakespeare course, but was put off when his university-trained daughter Sonia told him that he might have to tackle people like Chaucer in the original. Brainin, always game for new peaks to attempt, wonders whether he might, in due course, wield his fiddle and bow less and his pen more. He has in mind a semi-philosophical work, perhaps something on the Judaeo-Christian tradition and the ways it has issued in our present western culture. Whether he has his great-uncle Reuben's literary gifts remains to be seen, but it is hard to imagine Brainin producing anything dull.

For the time being, all of this is speculation. While the energies of all four players continue to be daunting by the standards of most mortals, prospects for the career of the Amadeus Quartet continue to look rosy. There are works to learn and re-learn, to perform and to record, and engagements to fulfil that are fixed two years or more ahead.

But one day it will all come to an end. If one player stops, they will all stop. 'As far as I am concerned,' says Nissel, and the others all concur, 'if something happened so that playing together was impossible, I would close up my quartet music and say "We have had a marvellous run, but *that's* the end." Teaching? Yes, that's OK. But I could not contemplate playing quartets with someone else. What for? To play worse than one's done so far? It couldn't be better. It could never be the same.'

He is right. It could never be the same. Few string quartets have equalled the musical standards of the Amadeus and none has maintained such standards for so long. And while the secret of the unmatched success of the Amadeus lies partly in the enormous talents of each of its four members, it rests ultimately in the unique chemistry whereby those four particular talents blend with one another to create a unity greater than the sum of its parts. Take away any one of those four elements and put in a substitute – of however high a calibre – and the ensemble as a whole would almost inevitably suffer. Norbert, Sigi, Peter and Martin all know this and have known it for a third of a century. Their audiences all over the world know it too. Which is why, for all the abnormal tensions some-times generated by the life they have chosen to lead, the members of the Amadeus Quartet continue to impose upon themselves an unending and punishing schedule of rehearsals, concerts, recordings and teaching engagements – two-thirds of them away from home. As the foursome gather up their instruments in one hand and their travel paraphernalia in the other and make their way across the tarmac of yet another airport at the start of yet another concert tour, they might contemplate the justice of Nissel's aphorism: it really *couldn't* be better. And how many people can look their life's achievements in the face and honestly say that?

"WELL IT'S EITHER ANOTHER UNSCHEDULED STOP IN CUBA, OR THAT'S
(EVENING STANDARD 9ᵗʰ SEPT. 1969) THE AMADEUS STRING QUARTET !"

SELECTIONS FROM THE AMADEUS DIARY *1979–1980*
AUTUMN 1979 EUROPEAN CONCERT TOUR

1979: September

21 Windsor	Schubert: op. 168
	Schubert: op. 163 (with William Pleeth)
23 Queen Elizabeth Hall, London	Mozart: K 156
	Mozart: K 493 (with Walter Klien)
	Mozart: K 478 (with Walter Klien)
	Mozart: K 465 (*Dissonance*)
24 Munich	Haydn: op. 76, No. 5
	Mozart: K 465 (*Dissonance*)
	Beethoven: op. 59, No. 2
25 Munich	Haydn: op. 76, No. 3
	Mozart: K 458 (*The Hunt*)
	Schubert: *Death and the Maiden*
27 Kaiserslautern	Schubert: op. 163 (with Jan Polacek)
29 Baden Weiler	Haydn: op. 54, No. 2
	Beethoven: op. 127
	Dvorak: op. 96 (*The American*)
30 Hamburg	Haydn: op. 64, No. 2
	Mozart: K 421
	Beethoven: op. 59, No. 3

October

1 Stuttgart	(radio concert) Schumann: op. 41, No. 3 Bartok: Quartet No. 6
3 Brunswick	Mozart: K 421 Schubert: *Quartettsatz* Beethoven: op. 59, No. 1
4 Hanover	Beethoven: op. 18, No. 4 Mozart: K 499 Dvorak: op. 96 (*The American*)
6 Kornwestheim	Haydn: op. 76, No. 3 Beethoven: op. 133 Schubert: *Death and the Maiden*
7 Würzburg	Beethoven: op. 18, No. 3 Smetana: Quartet No. 1 (*Aus Meinem Leben*) Haydn: op. 76, No. 1
8, 9 Cologne	Teaching
10 Brussels	Haydn: op. 76, No. 1 Mozart: K 465 (*Dissonance*) Beethoven: op. 127
11, 12 Cologne	Teaching
14 Norwich	Mozart: K 156 Britten: Quartet No. 3 Schubert: *Death and the Maiden*
15 Manchester	Mozart: K 458 Schumann: op. 41, No. 3 Schubert: *Death and the Maiden*
21 Royal Festival Hall, London	Brahms: op. 51, No. 2 Brahms: Piano Quintet (with Stephen Bishop-Kovacevich)
23–28 Munich	Record Tchaikovsky op. 11 and Verdi Quartet for Polydor

November

4 Lille   Haydn: *Seven Last Words*

6 Lille   Haydn: op. 64, No. 2
Mozart: K 465 (*Dissonance*)
Beethoven: op. 135

8 Amsterdam   Haydn: op. 64, No. 6
Beethoven: op. 95
Smetana: Quartet No. 1 (*Aus Meinem Leben*)

10 Amsterdam   Haydn: op. 64, No. 6
Beethoven: op. 95
Smetana: Quartet No. 1 (*Aus Meinem Leben*)

12–15 Cologne   Teaching

16 Vienna   Haydn: op. 76, No. 2
Mozart: K 387
Schubert: op. 29

19 Graz   Haydn: op. 76, No. 6
Schubert: op. 168
Mozart: K 421

21 Vienna   Haydn: op. 76, No. 3
Mozart: K 458
Schubert: op. 161

23 Vienna   Haydn: op. 76, No. 5
Schubert: op. 125, No. 1
Mozart: K 465 (*Dissonance*)

25 Vienna   Haydn: op. 76, No. 6
Schubert: op. 168
Mozart: K 421

27 Vienna   Haydn: op. 76, No. 4
Mozart: K 428
Schubert: op. 163 (with William Pleeth)

30 Vienna	Haydn: op. 76, No. 1
	Mozart: K 464
	Schubert: *Death and the Maiden*

December

1 Linz	Haydn: op. 76, No. 2
	Mozart: K 387
	Schubert: op. 29

1980 NORTH AMERICAN CONCERT TOUR

April

8 Charlottesville	Mozart: K 499 Bartok: Quartet No. 4 Smetana:Quartet No. 1
9 New York	Schubert: op. 168 Schubert: *Quartettsatz* Schubert: *Death and the Maiden*
10 New York	Haydn: op. 64, No. 6 Mendelssohn: op. 12, No. 1 Beethoven: op. 132
12 Vermont	Mozart: K 499 Britten: Quartet No. 3 Schubert: op. 29
13 Montreal	Haydn: op. 77, No. 1 Britten: Quartet No. 3 Schubert: *Death and the Maiden*
14 Buffalo	Beethoven: op. 18, No. 4 Beethoven: op. 135 Beethoven: op. 59, No. 2

16 Yale	Haydn: op. 64, No. 2
	Britten: Quartet No. 3
	Mozart: K 516
17 New York	Haydn: op. 74, No. 3
	Smetana: Quartet No. 1
	Dvorak: op. 96
18 Toronto	Haydn: op. 74, No. 3
	Britten: Quartet No. 2
	Dvorak: op. 96
20 Ann Arbor	Haydn: op. 76, No. 3
	Britten: Quartet No. 3
	Schubert: *Death and the Maiden*
21 Detroit	Brahms: op. 51, No. 2
	Brahms: op. 67
22 East Lansing	Haydn: op. 76, No. 3
	Britten: Quartet No. 3
	Beethoven: op. 127
24 Detroit	Brahms: op. 51, No. 1
	Brahms: Piano Quintet
26 Madison	Mozart: K 428
	Schubert: *Quartettsatz*
	Beethoven: op. 132
27 Lawrence, Kansas	Haydn: op. 64, No. 2
	Schubert: *Quartettsatz*
	Beethoven: op. 59, No. 1
28 Columbia, Missouri	Mozart: K 499
	Beethoven: op. 95
	Mendelssohn: op. 12, No. 1
30 Mozeman, Montana	Haydn: op. 76, No. 3
	Beethoven: op. 95
	Mendelssohn: op. 12, No. 1

May

2 Stanford   Haydn: op. 76, No. 3
                                    Britten: Quartet No. 3
                                    Dvorak: op. 96

3 La Jolla   Haydn: op. 76, No. 2
   Britten: Quartet No. 3
   Dvorak: op. 96

4 UCLA   Brahms: op. 51, No. 2
   Brahms: Piano Quintet

6 Vancouver   Mozart: K 421
   Britten: Quartet No. 3
   Beethoven: op. 127

7 Edmonton   Haydn: op. 76, No. 5
   Britten: Quartet No. 3
   Beethoven: op. 131

9 Davis   Haydn: op. 76, No. 5
   Bartok: Quartet No. 6
   Brahms: op. 51, No. 1

10 Santa Barbara   Haydn: op. 74, No. 1
   Bartok: Quartet No. 6
   Beethoven: op. 135

11 Pasadena   Mozart: K 590
   Britten: Quartet No. 3
   Beethoven: op. 131

THE REPERTOIRE

HAYDN	Op. 20 No. 5 in F minor	21 minutes
	Op. 33 No. 3 in C major	18
	Op. 54 No. 1 in G major	19
	Op. 54 No. 2 in C major	19
	Op. 55 No. 3 in B flat major	19
	Op. 64 No. 5 in D major (*The Lark*)	18
	Op. 64 No. 6 in E flat major	17
	Op. 74 No. 1 in C major	20
	Op. 74 No. 3 in G minor	20
	Op. 76 No. 1 in G major	21
	Op. 76 No. 2 in D minor	20
	Op. 76 No. 3 in C major (*Emperor*)	23
	Op. 77 No. 1 in G major	20

MOZART	K 387 in G major	26 minutes
	K 421 in D minor	24
	K 428 in E flat major	24
	K 458 in B flat major (*The Hunt*)	22
	K 465 in C major (*Dissonance*)	28
	K 499 in D major	30
	K 516 in G major	15

SCHUBERT	Op. 29 in A minor	31 minutes
	Op. Posth. in D minor (*Death and the Maiden*)	43
	Quartettsatz in C minor	10–12
	Op. 125 No. 1 in E flat major	28

BRAHMS	Op. 51 No. 1 in C minor	30 minutes
	Op. 51 No. 2 in A minor	31
	Op. 67 in B flat	34

BEETHOVEN	Op. 18 No. 1 in F major	25 minutes
	Op. 18 No. 2 in G major	22
	Op. 18 No. 3 in D major	20
	Op. 18 No. 4 in C major	20
	Op. 18 No. 5 in A major	25
	Op. 18 No. 6 in B flat major	24
	Op. 59 No. 1 in F major	45
	Op. 59 No. 2 in E minor	35
	Op. 59 No. 3 in C major	31
	Op. 74 in E flat major	31
	Op. 95 in F minor	21
	Op. 127 in E flat major	35
	Op. 130 in B flat major	35
	Op. 131 in C sharp minor	45
	Op. 132 in A minor	43
	Op. 133 in B flat major	16
	Op. 135 in F major	27

DVORAK	Op. 96 in F major (*The American*)	27 minutes

SMETANA	Quartet No. 1 (*Aus Meinem Leben*)	32 minutes

SCHUMANN	Op. 41 No. 3 in A major	28 minutes

MENDELSSOHN	Op. 12 No. 1 in E flat	24 minutes

CONTEMPORARY QUARTETS

BARTOK	Quartet No. 4	24 minutes
	Quartet No. 5	31
	Quartet No. 6	28

SEIBER	Quartet No. 3 (*Quartetto Lyrico*)	20 minutes

| BRITTEN | Quartet No. 2 | 27 minutes |
| | Quartet No. 3 | 28 |

| SHOSTAKOVICH | Quartet No. 13 | 22 minutes |

SUGGESTED PROGRAMMES 1977/78/79

Programme I

a. Any Haydn from Repertoire *or*
Any Mozart from Repertoire *or*
Schubert op. 125 No. 2 in E flat if no Schubert under
Section C
b. Any contemporary work from Repertoire

BRAHMS	c. Quartet in C minor op. 51 No. 1
BRAHMS	or Quartet in A minor op. 51 No. 2
BRAHMS	or Quartet in B flat major op. 67
SCHUMANN	or Quartet in A major op. 41 No. 3
DVORAK	or Quartet in F major op. 96
BEETHOVEN	or Quartet in F major op. 18 No. 1
BEETHOVEN	or Quartet in G major op. 18 No. 2
BEETHOVEN	or Quartet in D major op. 18 No. 3
BEETHOVEN	or Quartet in C minor op. 18 No. 4
BEETHOVEN	or Quartet in A major op. 18 No. 5
BEETHOVEN	or Quartet in B flat major op. 18 No. 6
BEETHOVEN	or Quartet in E minor op. 59 No. 2
BEETHOVEN	or Quartet in C major op. 59 No. 3
BEETHOVEN	or Quartet in E flat major op. 74
BEETHOVEN	or Quartet in F major op. 135
SCHUBERT	or Quartet in A minor op. 29
SCHUBERT	or Quartet in D minor op. Posth.

Programme II

a. Any Haydn from Repertoire *or*
Any Mozart from Repertoire

BRITTEN	b. Quartet No. 2
SEIBER	or Quartet No. 3
SHOSTAKOVICH	or Quartet No. 13
SCHUBERT	c. Quartet in D minor op. Posth.
BEETHOVEN	or Quartet in E flat major op. 127
BEETHOVEN	or Quartet in B flat major op. 130

133

Programme III

    a. Any Haydn from Repertoire *or*
        Schubert E flat op. 125 No. 2 (if not required under
        section C)
    b. Any Mozart from Repertoire *or*
        Schubert E flat op. 125 No. 2 (if not required under
        section C)
    c. As section C of Programme I

Programme IV

	a. Any Haydn from Repertoire
	or any Mozart from Repertoire
SCHUMANN	b. Quartet in A major op. 41 No. 3
SMETANA	or Quartet No. 1 (*Aus Meinem Leben*)
MENDELSSOHN	or Quartet in E flat op. 12 No. 1
BEETHOVEN	c. Quartet in F major op. 18 No. 1
BEETHOVEN	or Quartet in G major op. 18 No. 2
BEETHOVEN	or Quartet in D major op. 18 No. 3
BEETHOVEN	or Quartet in C minor op. 18 No. 4
BEETHOVEN	or Quartet in A major op. 18 No. 5
BEETHOVEN	or Quartet in B flat major op. 18 No. 6
BEETHOVEN	or Quartet in F minor op. 95
BEETHOVEN	or Quartet in F major op. 135

Programme V

	a. Any Haydn from Repertoire
	or any Mozart from Repertoire
BEETHOVEN	b. Quartet in F minor op. 95
BEETHOVEN	or Quartet in B flat major op. 133
BRAHMS	c. Quartet in C minor op. 51 No. 1
BRAHMS	or Quartet in A minor op. 51 No. 2
BRAHMS	or Quartet in B flat major op. 67
DVORAK	or Quartet in F major op. 96
SCHUMANN	or Quartet in A major op. 41 No. 3
SCHUBERT	or Quartet in D minor op. Posth.
SCHUBERT	or Quartet in A minor op. 29

Programme VI

	a. Any Haydn from Repertoire
	or any Mozart from Repertoire
SCHUBERT	b. Quartettsatz in C minor
BEETHOVEN	c. Quartet in F major op. 59 No. 1

BEETHOVEN	or Quartet in E flat major op. 127
BEETHOVEN	or Quartet in B flat major op. 130
BEETHOVEN	or Quartet in C sharp minor op. 131
BEETHOVEN	or Quartet in A minor op. 132
	or any other Beethoven Quartet

Programme VII

All-Beethoven programme to be chosen by the Organizers from the
Repertoire but to be approved by the Quartet.
Complete Beethoven Cycle in Six Programmes. Details given on request.
N.B.—Please avoid two works in the same key. All programmes chosen
subject to Quartet's approval.

Works with extra players:

6 Mozart Viola Quintets and Piano Quartets and Clarinet Quintet,
Oboe Quartet, Flute Quartets
Beethoven Viola Quintet
Brahms Quintets (Viola, Piano and Clarinet) and Sextets
Schumann Quintet
Schubert Quintet with cello and Trout Quintet
Brahms Piano Quartet in G minor

DISCOGRAPHY

Introductory note

All the recordings listed in the discography are on the Deutsche Grammophon label of the Polydor International GmbH except where otherwise stated. All recordings are listed in chronological order of date of recording by year, month and day(s) with the exception of the recordings made by the American Westminster label in the years 1950–51 where it has not been possible to find this data. I should like to express my warm thanks to EMI Ltd. and Polydor International GmbH for their co-operation in providing recording information.

MW

August 1980

Abbreviations

(m) denotes mono version
(4) denotes cassette version
* denotes 78rpm disc
(e) denotes electronically reprocessed stereo
nb: all recordings in stereo unless otherwise stated

1949 March 14. Decca Studios, 165 Broadhurst Gardens, London NW6
Rainier: String Quartet No. 1
$$AR13334^{-1-2-3}$$
Decca AK2278*

$$AR13335^{-1-2}$$
$$AR13336^{-1-2-3}$$
AK2279*

$$AR13337^{-1-2}$$

1950 May 15, 19 and 24. EMI Studio No. 3, Abbey Road, London NW6
Mozart: String Quartet No. 14 in G major, K 387
$$2EA14681^{-5}$$
C4014*

$$2EA14682^{-3}$$
$$2EA14683^{-1}$$
C4015*

$$2EA14684^{-1}$$
$$2EA14685^{-1}$$
C4016*

$$2EA14686^{-2}$$
$$2EA14687^{-1}$$
C4017* HMV (m) DLP1003
Victor (m) LHMV1039
Haydn: String Quartet No. 5 in F major, Op. 3 No. 5 – Serenade
$$2EA14688^{-1}$$
C4017*

1951 January 30–31 and February 2. EMI Studio No. 3
      Haydn: String Quartet No. 77 in C major, op. 76 No. 3
      2EA15365^{-4}
                                          C4066*

      2EA15366^{-5}
      2EA15367^{-3}
                                          C4067*

      2EA15368^{-3}
      2EA15369^{-1}
                                          C4068*

      2EA15370^{-3}
                                          Victor (m) LHMV1039

1951 January. Conway Hall, London
      Haydn: *Seven Last Words of Christ on the Cross,* op. 51
                                  Westminster (m) WL5064–5
                                           (m) XWN18055
                                  Nixa (m) WLP6202/1–2
      Haydn: String Quartet No. 83 in B flat major, op. 103
                                  Westminster (m) WAL202
                                           (m) WL5064
                                  Nixa (m) WLP6202/1–2
      Haydn: String Quartet No. 18 in F major, op. 3 No. 5
                                  Westminster (m) WAL202
                                           (m) WL5064
                                  Nixa (m) WLP6202/1–2
      Mozart: String Quartet No. 16 in E flat major, K 428
                                  Westminster (m) WL5099
                                  Nixa (m) WLP5099
                                  Westminster (m) XWN18557
      Mozart: String Quartet No. 17 in B flat major, K 458, *Hunt*
                                  Westminster (m) WL5099
                                  Nixa (m) WLP5099
                                  Westminster (m) XWN18557

1951 Konzerthaus, Vienna
      Brahms: String Quartet No. 1 in C minor, op. 51 No. 1
                                  Westminster (m) WL5084
                                           (m) XWN18440
      Mozart: String Quartet No. 18 in A major, K 464
                                  Westminster (m) WL5092
                                  Nixa (m) WLP5092
      Mozart: String Quartet No. 23 in F major, K 590
                                  Westminster (m) WL5092
                                  Nixa (m) WLP5092
                                  Westminster (m) XWN18560

Mozart: String Quintet No. 4 in G minor, K 516
with Cecil Aronowitz (viola II)
                                    Westminster (m) WL5086
                                    Nixa (m) WLP5086
                                    Westminster (m) XWN18036
Schubert: String Quartet No. 14 in C minor, D 703, *Quartetsatz*
                                    Westminster (m) WL5084
                                    Nixa (m) WLP5084
                                    Westminster (m) XWN18440

1951 September Beethovensaal, Hannover
      Schubert: String Quartet No. 15 in G major, D 887
                                    PV72132-4
                                    (m) LPM18010

1952 April 16-18 and 22-23. EMI Studio No. 3
      Schubert: String Quintet in C major, D 956
      with William Pleeth (cello II)
                                    HMV (m) CLP1006
                                    Victor (m) LHMV1051

1952 September 9-11. Decca Studios
      Mozart: Piano Quartets
      – No. 1 in G minor, K 478
      – No. 2 in E flat major, K 493
      with Sir Clifford Curzon (piano)
                                    Decca (m) LXT2722
                                    (e) ECS523
                                    London (m) LLP679
                                    (m) CM9061

1953 January 19. EMI Studio No. 1
      Mozart: Sinfonia Concertante in E flat major for violin, viola and
      orchestra, K 364
      Norbert Brainin (violin), Peter Schidlof (viola), London Mozart Players/
      Harry Blech
                                    HMV (m) CLP1014

1953 May 18-21. EMI Studio No. 3
      Schubert: String Quartet No. 14 in D minor, D 810 *Death and the Maiden*
                                    (m) LPM18191
                                    HMV (m) ALP1088
                                    Victor (m) LHMV1058

1953 October 2-3 and 5-6. EMI Studio No. 3
      Mozart: String Quintet No. 4 in C major, K 515
      with Cecil Aronowitz (viola II)
                                    LPM18240
                                    HMV (m) ALP1125 (T) HTB408

1954   May 4–6 and 15. Beethovensaal, Hannover
        Mozart: String Quartet No. 15 in D minor, K 421
                                    (m) LPM18201
                                    HMV (m) ALP1249
                                    Angel (m) 45024

1954   May 7–10. Beethovensaal, Hannover
        Haydn: String Quartet No. 58 in C major, op. 54 No. 2
                                    (m) LPM18201
                                    HMV (m) ALP1247
                                    Victor (m) 45024

1954   May 10–14. Beethovensaal, Hannover
        Schubert: String Quartet No. 13 in A minor, D 804
                                    LPM18294
                                    HMV (m) BLP1069
                                    Victor (m) LHMV27

1954   May 19, 21 and 24. EMI Studio No. 3
        Tippett: String Quartet No. 2
                                    HMV (m) ALP1302
                                    Argo (m) DA34

1954   May 23–24. EMI Studio No. 1
        Schubert: String Quartet in E flat major, D 87
                                    (m) LPM18527
                                    HMV (m) ALP1337
        Haydn: String Quartet No. 18 in A major, op. 20 No. 6 – Fuga con 3
        soggetti *only*
            2EA18000   HMS80*
                                    (m) HLP19
                                    Victor (m) LM6137

1954   May 24–25. EMI Studio No. 3
        Seiber: String Quartet No. 3
                                    HMV (m) ALP1302

1954   September 16–19. Beethovensaal, Hannover
        Mozart: String Quartet No. 19 in C major, K 465
                                    (m) LPM18242
                                    HMV (m) ALP1283 (T) HTA25
                                    Victor (m) LHMV32

1954   September 20–23. Beethovensaal, Hannover
        Mozart: String Quartet No. 21 in D major, K 575
                                    (m) LPM18242
                                    Victor (m) LHMV32
                                    HMV (m) ALP1283 (T) HTA25

141

1955   February 11–16. EMI Studio No. 1
Schubert: String Quartet No. 8 in B flat major, D 112
                              (m) LPM18527
                              HMV (m) ALP1673
Brahms: String Quartet No. 2 in A minor, op. 51 No. 2
                              (m) LPM18294
                              HMV (m) ALP1337
Mendelssohn: Four Pieces for string quartet, op. 81 – Capriccio and
Fugue in E minor
                              HMV (m) ALP1337
                              SLPM138527

1955   June 2–5. Studio Dr. Tienhaus, Hamburg
Mozart: String Quartet No. 20 in D major, K 499
                              (m) LPM18274
                              HMV (m) ALP1307

1955   June 5–7. Studio Dr. Tienhaus, Hamburg
Mozart: String Quartet No. 22 in B flat major, K 589
                              (m) LPM18274
                              HMV (m) ALP1307

1956   May 2–3. EMI Studio No. 1
Mozart: String Quartet No. 17 in B flat major, K 458
                              (m) LPM18368
                              HMV (m) ALP1488

1956   May 4–5. EMI Studio No. 1
Haydn: String Quartet No. 81 in G major, op. 77 No. 1
                              (m) LPM18368
                              HMV (m) ALP1488

1957   January 14–15
Haydn: String Quartet No. 57 in G major, op. 54 No. 1
                              (m) LPM18392/SLPM138071
                              HMV (m) ALP1579
                              Angel (m) 45024

1957   January 15–16. EMI Studio No. 1
Haydn: String Quartet No. 65 in B flat major, op. 64 No. 3
                              (m) LPM18392/SLPM138071
                              HMV (m) ALP1579

1957   March.   The Grenilla Arts Centre, London NW6
Beethoven: Eleven Waltzes – No. 1 in D major; No. 2 in B flat major;
No.3 in E flat major
with Norbert Brainin, Siegmund Nissel (violins), James W. Merrett
(double-bass), Richard Adeney, Lionel Solomon (flutes), Jack Brymer,
Stephen Waters (clarinets), Dennis Brain, Neil Sanders (horns)
Pye (m) CEC32027

1957   March 30–31 and April 10–11. EMI Studio No. 1
Brahms: String Quartet No. 3 in B flat major, op. 67
HMV (m) ALP1673
Mozart: String Quintet No. 6 in E flat major, K 614
with Cecil Aronowitz (viola II)
(m) LPM18398
HMV (m) ALP1539

1957   April 11–12 and 14. EMI Studio No. 1
Mozart: String Quintet No. 5 in D major, K 593
with Cecil Aronowitz (viola II)
(m) LPM18398/SLPM138057
HMV (m) ALP1539

1957   May 2–3. EMI Studio No. 1
Schubert: String Quartet No. 8 in B flat major, D 112
HMV (m) ALP1673

1957   May 22–24. Beethovensaal, Munich
Mozart: String Quartet No. 23 in F major, K 590
(m) LPM18399

1957   May 24–26. Beethovensaal, Munich
Mozart: String Quartet No. 16 in E flat major, K 428
(m) LPM18399

1957   October 21 and 23–24. EMI Studio No. 1
Haydn: String Quartet No. 74 in G minor, op. 74 No. 3, *Rider*
(m) LPM18495/SLPM138072
HMV (m) ALP1592

1957   October 24–26. EMI Studio No. 1
Haydn: String Quartet No. 72 in G major, op. 74 No. 1
(m) LPM18495/SLPM138072
HMV (m) ALP1592

1957   November 1–2. EMI Studio No. 1
        Mozart: String Quintet No. 4 in G minor, K 516
        with Cecil Aronowitz (viola II)
                                        SLPM138057
                                        HMV (m) BLP1105

1958   October 15–17
        Schubert: Piano Quintet in A major, D 667, *Trout*
        with Hephzibah Menuhin (piano) and James Edward Merrett (double-bass)
                                        HMV (m) ALP1733/ASD322
                                        Angel 35777/S35777

1959   April 3, 4 and 6. Beethovensaal, Hannover
        Schubert: String Quartet No. 14 in D minor, D 810, *Death and the Maiden*
                                (m) LPM18587/SLPM138048
                                2733 008
                                2535 314 (4) 3335 314

1959   April 8. Beethovensaal, Hannover
        Schubert: String Quartet No. 12 in C minor, D 703, *Quartetsatz*
                                (m) LPM18587/SLPM138048
                                2733 008
                                2535 314 (4) 3335 314

1959   May 19–27. Beethovensaal, Hannover
        Beethoven: String Quartets, op. 59, *Rasumovsky*
        – No. 7 in F major, op. 59 No. 1
        – No. 8 in E minor, op. 59 No. 2
        – No. 9 in C major, op. 59 No. 3
                                        (m) LPM18534–6/SLPM138534–6
                                        2721 071
                                        2721 130
                                        2733 005

1959   September 21–23. Beethovensaal, Hannover
        Brahms: String Quartet No. 2 in A minor, op. 51 No. 2
                                        (m) LPM18614/SLPM138114
                                        104 973–87
                                        2740 117
                                        2734 005

1959   September 23–24. Beethovensaal, Hannover
        Brahms: String Quartet No. 1 in C minor, op. 51 No. 1
                                        (m) LPM18614/SLPM138114
                                        104 973–87
                                        2740 117
                                        2734 005

144

1959   September 25–27. Beethovensaal, Hannover
        Dvořák: String Quartet No. 12 in F major, op. 96, *American*
                                    (m) LPM18626/SLPM138126

1960   January 11–13. Beethovensaal, Hannover
        Brahms: String Quartet No. 3 in B flat major, op. 67
                                    (m) LPM18626/SLPM138126
                                    104 973–87
                                    2740 117
                                    2734 005

1960   May 31–June 1. Beethovensaal, Hannover
        Beethoven: String Quartet No. 11 in F minor, op. 95
                                    (m) LPM18534–6/SLPM138534–6
                                    2721 071
                                    2721 130
                                    2733 005

1960   June 2–4. Beethovensaal, Hannover
        Beethoven: String Quartet No. 10 in E flat major, op. 74, *Harp*
                                    (m) LPM138534–6/SLPM138534–6
                                    2721 071
                                    2721 130
                                    2733 005

1961   September 6–24. Beethovensaal, Hannover
        Beethoven: String Quartets, op. 18
        – No. 1 in F major, op. 18 No. 1
        – No. 2 in G major, op. 18 No. 2
        – No. 3 in D major, op. 18 No. 3
        – No. 4 in C minor, op. 18 No. 4
        – No. 5 in A major, op. 18 No. 5
        – No. 6 in B flat major, op. 18 No. 6
                                    (m) LPM18531–3/SLPM138531–3
                                    2721 071
                                    2720 130
                                    2733 002

1962   April 7–12. Jesus Christuskirke, Berlin
        Beethoven: String Quartet No. 16 in A minor, op. 132
                                    (m) LPM18540/SLPM138540
                                    2721 071
                                    2720 130
                                    2733 002

1962   September 29–October 5. Jesus Christuskirke, Berlin
      Beethoven: String Quartet No. 13 in B flat major, op. 132
                         (m) LPM18538/SLPM138538
                         2721 071
                         2720 133
                         2734 066

1963   January
      Britten: String Quartet No. 2 in C major, op. 36
                         Argo (m) RG372/ZRG5372
                         Decca SXL6893
      Fricker: String Quartet No. 2, op. 20
                         Argo (m) RG372/ZRG5372

1963   March 29–April 4. UFA Studio, Berlin
      Beethoven: String Quartet No. 12 in E flat major, op. 127
                         LPM18537/SLPM138537
                         2734 006; 2721 071; 2721 130
      Beethoven: String Quartet No. 16 in F major, op. 135
                         LPM18537/SLPM138537
                         2734 006; 2721 071; 2721 130

1963   June 10–13. Beethovensaal, Hannover
      Beethoven: String Quartet No. 14 in C sharp minor, op. 131
                         (m) LPM18539/SLPM138539
                         2734 006; 2721 071; 2721 130

1963   June 18–19 and 23. Beethovensaal, Hannover
      Mozart: String Quartet No. 17 in B flat major, K 458, *Hunt*
                         (m) LPM18886/SLPM138886
                         2720 005; 2733 012

1963   June 20–22. Beethovensaal, Hannover
      Mozart: String Quartet No. 14 in G major, K 387
                         (m) LPM18909/SLPM138909
                         2720 005; 2733 012

1963   September 13–15. Beethovensaal, Hannover
      Haydn: String Quartet No. 77 in C major, op. 76 No. 3, *Emperor*
                         (m) LPM18886/SLPM138886 (4) 923 054
                         2734 001
      second movement *only*   2563 617

1964   March 21. Beethovensaal, Hannover
      Mozart: String Quartet No. 18 in A major, K 464
                         (m) LPM18909/SLPM138909
                         2733 012; 2720 055

1964　March 22. Beethovensaal, Hannover
Haydn: String Quartet No. 81 in G major, op. 77 No. 1
(m) LPM18980/SLPM138980
2734 001

1964　November 2–4. Beethovensaal, Hannover
Bruckner: String Quintet in F major
with Cecil Aronowitz (viola II)
(m) LPM18963/SLPM138963
2733 010

1964　December 20. BBC Studio No. 3, Maida Vale, London (broadcast
November 23, 1965)
Mozart: Violin Sonata No. 25 in F major, K 377
Norbert Brainin (violin), Lamar Crowson (piano)
BBC (m) REF313 (4) ZCD313

1964　December 22. BBC Studio No. 3, Maida Vale, London (broadcast
November 23, 1965)
Mozart: Violin Sonata No. 21 in E minor, K 304
Mozart: Violin Sonata No. 34 in A major, K 526
Norbert Brainin (violin), Lamar Crowson (piano)
BBC (m) REF313 (4) ZCD313

1965　March 3–4. Beethovensaal, Hannover
Haydn: String Quartet No. 82 in F major, op. 77 No. 2
(m) LPM18980/SLPM138980
2734 001

1965　March 4–7. Beethovensaal, Hannover
Schubert: String Quartet No. 15 in G major, D 887
139 103
2733 008

1965　April 13. BBC Studio No. 3, Maida Vale, London (broadcast December
12, 1965)
Mozart: Violin Sonata No. 24 in F major K 376
Norbert Brainin (violin), Lili Kraus (piano)
BBC (m) REF313 (4) ZCD313

1965　May 30–June 1. UFA Studio, Berlin
Schubert: String Quintet in C major, D 956
with William Pleeth (cello II)
139 105
2733 003; 2740 188

147

1966   Holland
Mozart: Sinfonia concertante in E flat major for violin, viola and orchestra, K 364
Norbert Brainin (violin), Peter Schidlof (viola), Netherlands Chamber Orchestra/David Zinman

HMV SXLP20112

1966   May 2–4. UFA Studio, Berlin
Mozart: String Quartet No. 16 in E flat major, K 428
139191
2734 001
Mozart: String Quartet No. 22 in B flat major, K 589
139191
2720 055; 2733 012
Haydn: String Quartet No. 76 in D minor, op. 76 No. 2
13919
2720 055; 2733 012

1966   May 20–23. UFA Studio, Berlin
Mozart: String Quartet No. 15 in D minor, K 421
139190
2720 055; 2733 012
Mozart: String Quartet No. 19 in C major, K 465, *Dissonance*
139190
2720 055; 2733 012

1966   May 23–27. UFA Studio, Berlin
Schubert: String Quartet No. 13 in A minor, D 804
139 194; 2733 008
Schubert: String Quartet No. 9 in G minor, D 173
139 194; 2733 008

1966   June 9. BBC Studio No. 2, Maida Vale, London (broadcast October 19, 1966)
Schubert: Sonatina No. 3 in G minor for violin and piano, D 408
Norbert Brainin (violin), Lili Kraus (piano)

BBC (m) REF313 (4) ZCD313

1966   October. Decca Studios
Holst: Four Songs for voice and violin, op. 35
Sir Peter Pears (tenor), Norbert Brainin (violin)

Argo (m) RG497
ZRG5497

148

1966   December 16–18. UFA Studio, Berlin
        Brahms: String Sextet No. 1 in B flat major, op. 18
        with Cecil Aronowitz (viola II), William Pleeth (cello II)
                                        139 353
                                        104 973–87; 2740 117; 2733 011

1967   March 16–19. UFA Studio, Berlin
        Brahms: Clarinet Quintet in B minor, op. 115
        with Karl Leister (clarinet)
                                        139 354
                                        104 973–87; 2740 117

1967   March 20. UFA Studio, Berlin
        Mozart: String Quartet No. 20 in D major, K 499
                                        139355
                                        2720 055

1967   May 16–20. UFA Studio, Berlin
        Mozart: String Quintet No. 3 in C major, K 515
        with Cecil Aronowitz (viola II)
                                        139356
                                        2709 056; 2740 122
        Brahms: String Quintet No. 2 in G major, op. 111
        with Cecil Aronowitz (viola II)
                                        104 973–87; 2740 117; 139 430;
                                        2733 011

1967   November 11. Memorial Hall, Farringdon Street, London (broadcast
        December 29, 1968)
        Beethoven: Violin Sonata No. 8 in G major, op. 30 No. 3
        Norbert Brainin (violin), Lili Kraus (piano)
                                        BBC (m) REF313 (4) ZCD313

1968   March 17–19. UFA Studios, Berlin
        Brahms: String Sextet No. 2 in G major, op. 36
        with Cecil Aronowitz (viola II), William Pleeth (cello II)
                                        104 973–87; 139459; 2740 011;
                                        2733 011

1968   March 20–22. UFA Studio, Berlin
        Mozart: String Quartet No. 23 in F major, K590, *Prussian*
                                        139437; 2720 055

1968   April 2–3. UFA Studio, Berlin
        Mozart: String Quartet No. 6 in E flat major, K 614
        with Cecil Aronowitz (viola II)
                                        139433; 2709 056; 2740 122

1968　April 4–6. UFA Studio, Berlin
Brahms: String Quintet No. 1 in F major, op. 88
with Cecil Aronowitz (viola II)

104 973–87; 139430; 2740 117;
2733 011

1968　April 7–8. UFA Studio, Berlin
Mozart: String Quintet No. 5 in D major, K 593
with Cecil Aronowitz (viola II)

139433; 2709 056; 2740 122

1968　May 29–31. UFA Studio, Berlin
Brahms: Piano Quintet in F minor, op. 34
with Christoph Eschenbach (piano)

104 973–87; 139397; 2740 117

1969　January 27–30. UFA Studio, Berlin
Beethoven: String Quintet in C major, op. 29
with Cecil Aronowitz (viola II)

643 627; 2721 130

Beethoven: String Quartet based on the Piano Sonatas in E major, op. 14
No. 1

643 627; 2721 130

1969　April 19–22. UFA Studio, Berlin
Mozart: String Quartet No. 21 in D major, K 575, *Prussian*

139437; 2720 055

Mozart: Horn Quintet in E flat major, K 407
with Gerd Seifert (horn)

2530 012; 2733 013

1969　June 11–13. St. Michaels Heim, Berlin
Beethoven: Piano Quartets, Woo36
– No. 1 in E flat major
– No. 2 in D major
– No. 3 in C major
with Christoph Eschenbach (piano)

643 661; 2721 174; 2535 174
(4) 3335 174

1970　March 8–10. St. Michaels Heim, Berlin
Haydn: String Quartet No. 75 in G major, op. 76 No. 1

2530 089; 2734 001; 2535 169 (4)
3335 169

Haydn: String Quartet No. 78 in B flat major, op. 76 No. 4, *L'Aurore*

2530 089; 2734 001

1970   May 28–31. Studio Lankwitz, Berlin
Haydn: String Quartet No. 79 in D major, op. 76 No. 5
2530 072; 2734 001
Haydn: String Quartet No. 80 in E flat major, op. 76 No. 6
2530 072; 2734 001

1970   December 21–22. Bavaria Atelier, Munich
Brahms: Piano Quartet No. 1 in G minor, op. 25
with Emil Gilels (piano)
2530 133; 2542 140; (4) 3342 140

1971   May 19–21. Phonga Studio, Lindau, Zurich
Haydn: *Seven Last Words of Christ on the Cross,* op. 51
2530 213

1971   October 19–21. Plenarsaal, Munich
Haydn: String Quartet No. 57 in G major, op. 54 No. 1
2530 302
Haydn: String Quartet No. 58 in C major, op. 54 No. 2
2530 302

1973   March 3–6. Plenarsaal, Munich
Haydn: String Quartet No. 65 in B flat major, op. 64 No. 3
2740 107
Haydn: String Quartet No. 66 in G major, op. 64 No. 4
2740 107
Haydn: String Quartet No. 83 in B flat major, op. 103
awaiting release

1973   December 8–11. Plenarsaal, Munich
Haydn: String Quartet No. 63 in C major, op. 64 No. 1
2740 107
Haydn: String Quartet No. 64 in D major, op. 64, No. 2
2740 107

1974   March 27–30. Plenarsaal, Munich
Haydn: String Quartet No. 67 in D major, op. 64 No. 5
2740 107
Haydn: String Quartet No. 68 in E flat major, op. 64 No. 6
2740 107

1974   September 25–29. Schonburg Palace, Vienna
Mozart: String Quartet No. 1 in G major, K 80
2711 020; 2740 165
Mozart: Divertimento No. 1 in D major, K 136
2711 020; 2740 165
Mozart: Divertimento No. 2 in B flat minor, K 138
2711 020; 2740 165
Mozart: Divertimento No. 3 in F major, K 138
2711 020; 2740 165
Mozart: String Quintet No. 1 in B flat major, K 174
with Cecil Aronowitz (viola II)
2709 056; 2740 122

1975   March 18. Walthamstow Town Hall, London
Mozart: String Quartet No. 5 in D major, K 593 – Fourth movement
(original version)
with Cecil Aronowitz (viola II)
2709 056; 2740 122

1975   August 31–September 4. Turku Concert House, Finland
Schubert: Piano Quintet in A major, D 667, *Trout*
with Emil Gilels (piano) and Rainer Zepperitz (double-bass)
2530 646 (4) 3300 646
2536 381 (4) 3336 381
2740 188

1975   December 1–12. Alter Herkulessaal, Munich
Mozart: Clarinet Quintet in A major, K 581
with Gervase de Peyer (clarinet)
2530 720 (4) 3300 720
Mozart: Oboe Quartet in F major, K 370
with Lothar Koch (oboe)
2530 720 (4) 3300 720
Mozart: String Quartet No. 2 in D major, K 155
2711 020; 2740 165
Mozart: String Quartet No. 3 in G major, K 156
2711 020; 2740 165
Mozart: String Quartet No. 4 in C major, K 157
2711 020; 2740 165
Mozart: String Quartet No. 5 in F major, K 158
2711 020; 2740 165

1976   June 6–11. Alter Herkulessaal, Munich
        Mozart: String Quartet No. 6 in B flat major, K 159
                                2711 020; 2740 165
        Mozart: String Quartet No. 7 in E flat major, K 160
                                2711 020; 2740 165
        Mozart: String Quartet No. 8 in F major, K 168
                                2711 020; 2740 165
        Mozart: String Quartet No. 9 in A major, K 169
                                2711 020; 2740 165

1976   September 14–18. Alter Herkulessaal, Munich
        Mozart: String Quartet No. 10 in C major, K 170
                                2711 020; 2740 165
        Mozart: String Quartet No. 11 in E flat major, K 171
                                2711 020; 2740 165
        Mozart: String Quartet No. 12 in B flat major, K 172
                                2711 020; 2740 165
        Mozart: String Quartet No. 13 in D minor, K 173
                                2711 020; 2740 165

1977   June 5–7. Alter Herkulessaal, Munich
        Haydn: String Quartet No. 69 in B flat major, op. 71 No. 1
                                2709 090
        Haydn: String Quartet No. 70 in B flat major, op. 71 No. 2
                                2709 090
        Beethoven: Grosse Fuge No. 16 in F major, op. 133
                                awaiting release
        Beethoven: String Quartet No. 16 in F major, op. 135
                                awaiting release

1977   June 26–30. Savonlinna Festival, Finland
        Smetana: String Quartet No. 1 in E minor, *From my Life*
                                2530 994
        Dvořák: String Quartet No. 12 in F major, op. 96, *American*
                                2530 994

1977   July 22–25. Savonlinna Festival, Finland
        Mozart: Flute Quartets
        – No. 1 in D major, K 285
        – No. 2 in G major, K 285a
        – No. 3 in C major, K Anh. 171
        – No. 4 in A major, K 298
        with Andreas Blau (flute)
                                2530 983; (4) 3300 983

153

1977   September 28–30. The Maltings, Snape, Suffolk – Benson and Hedges
        Music Festival
        Schubert: Piano Quintet in A major, D 667, *Trout* – Theme and
        Variations
        with Sir Clifford Curzon (piano), Rodney Slatford (double-bass)
        Schubert: String Quintet in C major, D 956 – Adagio and Scherzo
        with William Pleeth (cello II)
        Schubert: String Quartet No. 12 in D minor, D 703, *Quartettsatz*
        Schubert: String Quartet No. 8 in B flat major, D 112 – Minuet and Trio
                          CBS (UK) 79316
                          (US) M3-35197

1978   January 2–4. Alter Herkulessaal, Munich and
1978   December 5 and 8. Plenarsaal, Munich
        Haydn: String Quartet No. 71 in E flat major, op. 71 No. 3
                    2709 090
        Haydn: String Quartet No. 72 in C major, op. 74 No. 1
                    2709 090
        Haydn: String Quartet No. 73 in F major, op. 74 No. 2
                    2709 090
        Haydn: String Quartet No. 74 in G minor, op. 74 No. 3
                    2709 090

1978   March. The Maltings, Snape, Suffolk
        Britten: String Quartet No. 3, op. 94
                        Decca SXL6895

1978   November 2–10. Plenarsaal, Munich
        Beethoven: String Quartet No. 12 in E flat major, op. 127
                    awaiting release
        Mozart: Adagio and Fugue in C minor, K 546
                    awaiting release

1979   April 29–May 2. Plenarsaal, Munich
        Mozart: Serenade No. 13 in G major, K 525, *Eine kleine Nachtmusik*
        with Rainer Zepperitz (double-bass)
                    2531 253
        Mozart: *A Musical Joke,* K 522
        with Rainer Zepperitz (double-bass), Gerd Seifert and Manfred Klier
        (horns)
                    2531 253

1979   October 24–28. Alter Herkulessaal, Munich
        Tchaikovsky: String Quartet No. 1 in D major, op. 11
                2531 283 (4) 3301 283
        Verdi: String Quartet in E minor
                2531 283 (4) 3301 283

1980   January 16–21. Plenarsaal, Munich
          Beethoven: String Quartet No. 15 in A minor, op. 132
                               awaiting release

Compiled by Malcolm Walker with thanks to Alfred Kaine, Juliane Griebel and Steven Paul.

INDEX

ACKNOWLEDGMENTS

Acknowledgment is made to the following for permission to reproduce illustrative material: the Britten Estate (page 45); the Dartington Hall Trust (pages 33, 34); the *Evening Standard* (page 122); Professor Robert Cahn (page 25).

The examples of music are reproduced by courtesy of Ernst Eulenberg Ltd.

The limerick on page 91 is taken from *The Devil's Own Song and Other Verses* by Lord Hailsham, and reproduced by permission of the publishers Hodder & Stoughton. The quotation from an article by Andrew Porter on pages 111–12 appears by permission of *The New Yorker* magazine.